A

Protected Killer

VERA SHILLING

Dedicated to my late partner Terry. Dog Warden for many years and the inspiration behind some of the incidents described in the book.

TABLE OF CONTENTS

PROLOGUE

Imagine if you discovered that your mother, father, sister, brother, best friend was a killer.

Would you turn them in?

Now imagine that by turning them in, they would face certain death for the crime they had committed.

Would you still turn them in?

Would you? Really?

Look around you.

Who or what can you see?

The fact that makes this story so horrific is that one of you who is reading this is probably looking at the next hidden killer right now.

CHAPTER 1
VICTORIA'S STORY

Victoria woke to the sound of screams, dripping in cold sweat and a pounding headache. She managed to move her body and rolled over to look at the clock. *Five thirty,* she sighed. The alarm was set for six thirty, but there was no chance Tommy was going back to sleep now and if left alone, he would wake the girls and the chaos would ensue.

Victoria decided to get up, neglecting her body aches. She straightened her body to get relief from the pain, wrapped herself in her old faded dressing gown and hurried to Tommy's bedroom.

Tommy was screaming at the top of his lungs—a high-pitched, ear-piercing scream that sounded more like an animal in pain than a crying baby. He was now a two-year-old baby, but Victoria had suspected something was awry with Tommy from the time he was born, as he was nothing like her older children. Laura had been an easy baby who rarely cried. Shelly was more fretful and would cry for the least reason. Wind, a slightly wet nappy, the sun in her eyes, but there was always a reason and Victoria had always been able to calm her.

But Tommy was different. He would scream, really loudly and for no apparent reason. His screams could empty a shop in two seconds flat. A beautiful little blond baby with a kiss curl, which made him a completely adorable child until he opened his mouth. She missed the cute gurgles her other babies used to make, even the cute 'Da Da' as they started to talk, but for now, she only had to hear screams.

At first, Victoria wondered if it was just that he was a boy. Perhaps baby boys were more difficult to care for because she had never raised a boy, as her first children were girls.

Her partner Jeff struggled with the newborn Tommy as he used to share their bedroom and slept in a cot close to their bed. But Tommy would wake up like an alarm clock for a night feed without any warning. There was no gentle tossing and turning before he woke. He would just open his eyes and scream.

"Jesus Christ!" Jeff would say. "For God's sake, do something with him."

Victoria would jump out of bed grabbing Tommy and doing her best to calm him. He would always wake the neighbors with his loud shriek as if he was in pain. Victoria even bought an expensive bottle heater so that the bottle would be ready the instant Tommy woke up. But the sudden onset of screaming in the middle of the night was more than Jeff could cope with. And the worst part was that Tommy would frequently wake the girls, turning the peaceful nights into chaos. Victoria would always try her best to calm

Tommy and persuade the girls to go back to sleep rather than having a mid-night toy party.

Often, the girls insisted on coming downstairs so Victoria would make hot chocolate and try to quieten the noisy house so that Jeff could get some sleep before heading off to work. Laura and Shelly were just five and six. They, too, had to get up in the morning and go to school. One day, Shelly had fallen asleep with her head on her desk. Victoria had been spoken to by a very unsympathetic teacher who told her that it was important for Shelly to get her proper sleep. Victoria tried to explain but the teacher said, "You should respond to the baby more quickly before he had the chance to disturb Shelly." Victoria had been exhausted. The house was a mess. She was a bigger mess.

Once, Victoria used to be slim, attractive and energetic. But since Tommy, she has become too skinny. Her hourglass shape had disappeared. Her shapely legs resembled matchsticks, and her oversized clothes hung on her thin frame.

She took Tommy to the doctor, but he didn't seem interested. He declared that Tommy was a healthy baby, just a little on the loud side, and prescribed anti-depressants for Victoria.

Victoria took the tablets for a couple of weeks but quickly realized the effect was to make her even more tired and consequently less able to cope. She became short-tempered and the arguments between Jeff and herself got worse.

Looking back, Victoria wondered if she could have done anything differently. She loved Jeff, but in the end, it felt as if she had been forced into a choice between the man she loved and her baby. Jeff was a wonderful father to the girls and tried his best with Tommy, but his screams would always test his father's patience.

Victoria's world collapsed when she returned from dropping the girls at school to find Jeff's letter on the kitchen table. He explained that he had gone to stay with his mother. He said he could not cope with the lack of sleep and her refusal to discipline Tommy. *Discipline?* she thought. Tommy was just over twelve months old. *How on earth can you discipline a baby that young?* But Jeff accused Victoria of giving Tommy a free hand—picking him up too much and rushing to his side, leaving everything the moment Tommy would wake up. Cooking, cleaning, and even making love were abandoned as soon as he screamed. Jeff said she favored Tommy and that he and the girls felt pushed aside. Jeff's letter said he was fed up with living in a hovel with a woman who couldn't be bothered to keep herself clean.

Victoria was hurt. She knew that Tommy's high-pitched screams were unbearable to the family, so she did everything she could to placate him as quickly as possible.

Even next door, old Mrs Thomas complained about Tommy's constant screams. Mrs Thomas was well into her eighties and quite deaf. But she had been in the garden one day when Tommy had started one of his frequent screaming episodes. Mrs Thomas, who never commented on anything, tutted and said, "I couldn't put up with that if he were mine."

To begin with, Jeff had visited frequently and Victoria had hoped he would return. But Tommy's behaviour hadn't improved and even Jeff's visits became fraught. Eventually, he agreed to take the girls out on a Saturday morning, but not Tommy. Tommy never seemed to respond or acknowledge him, so Jeff gave up and ignored him.

Victoria had so badly wanted Jeff to come home. She still loved him and missed him. But she never seemed to have time to make herself presentable before he came to visit. She knew she looked unattractive and dirty with shaggy clothes and messy hair. She knew how Jeff eyed her with disgust and seemed unable to speak more than a few words to her. She had changed so much from the day they got married. How could he love her now?

She tried to accept that this was now her life. She settled into a routine and felt like a robot. She couldn't cry or laugh. She made meals for her children and made sure they had clean clothes. She hugged them and kissed them goodnight. She loved them, but it was a tired love. When she kissed them goodnight, she felt relief that another day was over and she hoped for a few hours rest before the next day.

So here she was at five-thirty in the morning, with a screaming Tommy in her arms. She rushed downstairs in an attempt to reach the living room and close the door before the girls woke up. She tripped on an abandoned doll and almost fell through the door, closing it rapidly behind her.

Made it. No sound from upstairs. The girls were still asleep.

The old Spaniel, Ruby, stirred in her bed and pottered to the door. She was a calm and well-mannered dog with a thick, fluffy coat and cute puppy eyes that would melt anyone's heart. She was disciplined and used to the routine. Victoria sometimes thought there must be something wrong with her hearing. *Aren't dogs supposed to be driven mad by high-pitched sounds?* But Ruby was the only one that ever seemed to calm Tommy. Ruby and Tommy seemed to have an understanding. So Ruby went out for her usual morning pee but returned quickly as if she knew that Tommy needed her, so she didn't sniff around as you would expect from a dog. She simply did a pee and rushed back in.

Victoria sat Tommy on the floor next to Ruby, and the two snuggled together. Tommy stopped screaming. "Wuby!" Tommy said in a sweet, angelic voice.

Tommy was slow to walk and talk. At two, most toddlers started to string words together and potter around, but he would say very few words and refuse to learn any. He would point if he wanted something and if it didn't arrive promptly, the screaming would start again. But he would always respond to Ruby. He never pulled her fur or her tail. *Wuby* was the first word he had said. Not *Da Da*, like most babies. In fact, Victoria was worried that he may not speak at all. He seemed disinterested in mimicking sounds. Then, one day, he was sat next to the dog, and the only word he uttered was *Wuby*. The word seemed adorable coming from Tommy. He said "Wuby" again in his sweet, angelic voice. They all sat quietly together while Victoria prepared a milk bottle for Tommy. Peace.

Victoria laid Tommy on his back with his bottle and changed his nappy without moving him too far from Ruby. Ruby placid as ever, looked on. Ruby was seven so had been around before any of the children were born. They did not plan on making Ruby a part of their family. Victoria and Jeff had been visiting friends whose dog had recently had puppies and they had both fallen in love with Ruby and agreed instantly to home her.

As soon as she had been weaned, they brought her home. She had never been any trouble. She was quick and easy to housetrain and seemed calmer than most other spaniels. Ruby was inquisitive, gently sniffing at new objects. She didn't bound around even as a young dog. She never strayed too far when out walking, always returned when called and never snatched at food.

Jeff commented that she must have been trained in a former life.

When Victoria brought her first baby home Ruby strolled over, inquisitive as ever. Victoria, slightly nervous and thinking that Ruby may be jealous held Laura close to her. But she needn't have bothered. Ruby sniffed then wandered off and laid down.

It wasn't long before Victoria trusted Ruby completely and when Shelly arrived Ruby accepted her into the family with the usual sniff, then disinterest.

As the girls grew, they dressed Ruby in their dolls clothes, pushed her around in the pram and insisted that she attend their teddy bears picnic. Ruby never seemed to mind. If the play got rough, Ruby would do her best to remove herself. There was never any sign of aggression. In fact, Jeff or Victoria would come to Ruby's rescue when it was obvious that the poor dog had been subjected to quite enough play.

"Leave that poor dog alone," Jeff would say. "I'm sure she doesn't want to be tied into a baby's bonnet."

But when Tommy arrived Ruby behaved differently. It was partially Ruby's reaction to Tommy that made Victoria think there was something more to Tommy's behaviour than simply a difficult baby.

Dogs know things, Victoria had thought to herself.

Ruby hung around Tommy, almost as if she was guarding him. She would affectionately lick his hand or nudge him with her nose. She had an instant and calming effect on Tommy. Ruby seemed to provide the only respite Victoria had.

It was clear that there was an inexplicable bond between Tommy and Ruby. Sometimes, when Victoria picked Tommy up, he would scream and wriggle until she put him back on the floor next to Ruby. Victoria felt a sense of jealousy, but she told herself that was ridiculous yet was glad that Tommy had found someone in his life that seemed to release him from his hidden torment.

Tommy's screams sounded like he was being tortured. It left Victoria anxious and desperate. She was unable to help her baby boy. She was convinced that there was something wrong, but what?

There was no one to turn to and no one able to help.

Victoria's father had left the family home when he met a rich American woman. Victoria was just nine and her sister was eleven. She saw very little of her father after he left. Victoria's mother refused to talk about him.

Victoria's sister was the apple of her mother's eye and Victoria lived in her shadow. She went to university and married a man who ran a successful technology business.

Victoria scored average grades at school and got hired in an office on average pay. She had several boyfriends before Jeff, but Jeff was her first serious boyfriend. There had never been anyone like Jeff and Victoria didn't believe there ever could be anyone else. They married just six months after their first date.

Victoria's mother didn't even try to disguise her disapproval. She took every opportunity to compare Victoria to her sister and Jeff to her sister's husband. When Victoria became pregnant, her mother told her she was not ready to be a grandmother and hoped that the baby wouldn't turn out like Jeff, such a 'no-hoper.' At that point, Victoria decided that she didn't want her mother in her life. It was bad enough that she faced her mother's continual criticism, but worse that she could think so badly of Jeff and unspeakable that she could think badly of her unborn grandchild. So when Laura was born, Victoria didn't phone her mother with the news. Once or twice, she had seen her mother in town. They had even exchanged pleasantries like, "How are things? How's Jeff?" But neither wanted to take the conversation further. So, any exchange was usually cut short by "Must dash, appointment," and they would part with a sigh of relief.

When Jeff left, Victoria thought briefly about getting in touch with her mother but quickly dismissed the idea. Her mother would probably gloat, and any help would surely be met with "I told you so" or just a smug look. *No,* Victoria thought. *Better on my own.* But there didn't seem to be any way out. Everything felt such a mess. Her marriage, her home, she herself—broken, discarded, numb.

Then, one insignificant day, it all changed. A dull, cloudy day where everything felt grey and lifeless. But it was a day which Victoria would come to remember as a day full of brightness and sunshine. Because it was the day she met Becky. Becky, who turned Victoria's life around.

Victoria had been picking the girls up from school when Tommy started another screaming fit. A young mum whom Victoria hadn't seen before had glanced in her direction and smiled.

"Difficult, isn't it?" she said sympathetically. "My sister's got one like that, but she's getting help now."

Victoria seemed to latch on to the word 'help' as if it was the only word the woman had said.

"What do you mean by help, eh?"

"Well, since the diagnosis, she's had more help."

Victoria looked at the woman. She was casually dressed in jeans and a teeshirt with a mop of blond curls that bounced with each movement. She had a round face and an appealing smile, which made Victoria feel dowdy and dirty by comparison. Victoria hadn't found time to wash her hair so she had pulled her once shiny brunette tresses into a tight ponytail. It felt greasy and the straggly ends clung to her neck. Her jeans were too big. Money was tight and although Jeff did give her some, he wasn't well paid. He had to pay housekeeping to his mother and taking the girls out every Saturday was costing money too. Jeff's refusal to sit in the house with Tommy screaming meant that he had to take the girls to the swimming pool, cinema or other exorbitant entertainment, so he paid Victoria whatever he could. Victoria struggled to balance the household budget. She certainly had no spare money to buy clothes. She had recently purchased a new coat from a second-hand shop and felt instantly guilty. The children always needed something, so it seemed wrong to spend even a small amount of money on herself.

Victoria had changed from a vibrant, pretty brunette with a cracking figure into a thin, dreary thing with bags under her eyes and no interest in improving her appearance. She looked at this strange pretty person, wondering why ever anyone would want to pass the time of day with her. Surely, this attractive woman wouldn't want to be seen with someone like her. This woman would have her own circle of nice friends with nice houses and nice husbands. But her comment intrigued Victoria. *One like that. Did she see something in Tommy that other people had missed? Were there others like Tommy?*

"What do you mean?" asked Victoria, not really expecting an answer.

"Autistic," said the woman in a matter-of-fact tone. "My sister's girl is autistic, too."

"But Tommy isn't autistic," said Victoria.

"Oh, I'm so sorry." said the woman. "I just thought… well, it was the scream, you see. That's very typical of autistic children, so I just thought. Oh well, I'm so sorry. Sometimes I feel like I've got size ten feet." She was obviously embarrassed and blushed profusely as she attempted to move away.

"No, wait," Victoria grabbed her arm. "Please," Victoria was almost begging.

Becky turned, and she looked uncertain, but then she smiled. "I'm Becky," said the woman. "I've just moved into Covent Close."

"Oh!" said Victoria. "That's just around the corner from me. I live in Castle Road."

Becky smiled her appealing smile. "I didn't mean to offend you. I just thought with that scream."

"You didn't offend me," said Victoria. "I've been really struggling. I can't get anyone to take me seriously, but I often think something's wrong."

At that moment, Victoria's exhaustion and despair seemed to overtake her and tears filled her eyes.

"It's okay," said Becky sympathetically. "My sister went through the same. Her little girl was misdiagnosed for ages. I hope I'm wrong, but it's that scream. It just sounds the same as my sister's little one. Please don't be offended, but I thought…"

At that moment Tommy's screaming stopped as abruptly as it started. There was never any slowing down with Tommy. He was either screaming or completely switched off, showing very little interest in the world around him; some things would seem to amuse him for a while. He would see a shape or hear a noise, but it seemed random. The only thing that guaranteed his interest was Ruby.

The women continued to chat as they walked home with the children. Becky had a girl the same age as Shelly. They were in the same class and had made friends earlier in the day. Victoria felt a weight being lifted from her. She was doing something normal, enjoying the company of another adult. The girls were laughing and were happy as Tommy quietly looked around the place lost in his own thoughts.

As they chatted, Becky told Victoria everything she knew about autism. The more Victoria listened, the more convinced she became that the description matched Tommy's behavior exactly.

Victoria told Becky about Tommy's behavior and how it had become unbearable for Jeff. She told Becky how alone she felt. As they parted, Becky told Victoria that she would help in any way she could.

As Victoria pushed open her garden gate, Tommy's screams started again, but somehow, it didn't seem quite so bad. *Could there be some hope at last?* She saw Ruby waiting by the door.

The next morning, Victoria phoned her doctor's surgery as soon as it opened. She was eleventh in the queue. *How can that happen?* she thought to herself. *What do you have to do to be first in the queue?*

A bored-sounding receptionist answered the phone and offered a telephone consultation at three in the afternoon. "That's no good," stated Victoria. "I will be picking my children up from school at three and anyway, I want to see the doctor in person."

"We haven't got any physical appointments left," drawled the receptionist.

"Well, it's like this," said Victoria in a strong voice, much stronger than she felt. "My little boy needs to see a doctor. And if you don't give me an appointment, I will simply come to the surgery and refuse to move until he is seen."

The newfound hope had given Victoria a strength which had alluded her since Tommy was born. She smiled to herself as she recognized a glimpse of the woman she had once been. After a pause and some shuffling of paper, the receptionist, in a curse voice, said, "Dr. Jones, eleven o'clock." She put the phone down without waiting for Victoria's response.

Victoria met Becky by the school gate and excitedly told her about the appointment. "It's a start," said Becky. "But getting a diagnosis is an uphill battle."

Victoria's smile faded and replaced it with a frown, which stayed till her eyes met Tommy's. She faked a smile at Tommy, who was busy playing with Ruby.

"I'll come with you if you like," said Becky to comfort her.

Victoria felt a sense of relief and gratitude. This woman, who she barely knew, was giving her the support and friendship that was so needed. They arranged that Becky would come to Victoria's house while she changed Tommy and got ready for the appointment. Tommy started screaming as if in pain as soon as Victoria tried changing his bodysuit, but Ruby was always there to rescue him. She came in and comforted Tommy.

"It's weird," said Victoria. "Ruby is the only thing that stops Tommy from screaming. They seem to have a special bond."

Becky bent to stroke Ruby. "So what are you going to do with the puppies?"

Victoria's face was a picture of complete horror, as if she had seen a ghost.

"You knew, right?" said Becky, looking at Victoria with a quizzical look.

Victoria's mind was racing. Ruby never went out alone. But there had been one instance on a hot day when Victoria had left Ruby in the garden rather than lock her in the house.

It was only for half an hour while she went to pick up the girls. When Victoria returned she had found a large white dog in the garden with Ruby. They appeared to be playing so Victoria had simply shooed the dog out of the garden and thought no more of it.

"Are you sure?" Victoria said, sounding horrified.

"Well, something moved in there," said Becky. "And I don't think it's wind."

What now, thought Victoria, feeling panic and a wave of nausea.

"Do you have to take a pregnant dog to the vet?" Victoria could barely afford her food bill and now puppies. Victoria couldn't even think of having puppies in her home. As for the pregnancy, animals usually manage well enough on their own. Ruby would have to take her chances. Today, she needed to concentrate on Tommy and his needs. Pregnant dogs and puppies would just have to wait.

The doctor faced the two women across the consulting room. They were an intimidating team. One seemed to have extensive knowledge of autism. The mother, who he remembered as a quiet, retiring young woman, seemed to have developed a new character, like a lion defending her cub. She spoke clearly and in a voice that commanded attention.

The doctor tried to engage Tommy in a game, rattling his keys and clapping his hands. Tommy stared blankly ahead. Having listened to Victoria's description of Tommy's development and behaviour, he said that Tommy should be referred to a specialist. He agreed that Tommy was indeed showing signs of autism.

Victoria should have felt dismayed. Instead, she felt elated. At last, she knew that her inability to cope wasn't because she lacked the parental skills needed. It was because Tommy had a condition that made his behaviour enough to challenge any parent. Finally, Victoria was able to believe that she wasn't a failure.

Over the next few weeks. Tommy saw two other doctors and was given a firm diagnosis. A health visitor came and offered a nursery place that could help with Tommy's development and give Victoria some much-needed time of her own.

Ruby's condition was at the back of Victoria's mind, but now Victoria started to feel on top of her problems and didn't dwell on negative thoughts. She felt more energetic. She started to wear a bit of makeup and bought herself some tight-fitting second-hand jeans. She wore her hair down and when she caught sight of herself in the mirror, there was a resemblance to the young woman she used to be. Tommy didn't seem quite so draining. She stood next to the other mothers when she went to pick the girls up from school.

People seemed to have a new understanding now that Tommy's behaviour could be explained. Life felt easier.

When Victoria descended one morning with Tommy in her arms, she felt surprised and dismayed to see that Ruby had given birth to three squirming puppies. Ruby lay quietly and lifted her head when Victoria came into the room. There was blood in Ruby's bed and Victoria wondered if this was normal, but apart from fatigue, Ruby seemed okay.

When the girls awoke, Victoria told them about the new arrivals. The girls wanted to see the puppies, so Victoria allowed them a brief visit but told them Ruby needed rest.

After dropping the girls at school, she allowed Tommy to sit with Ruby and the puppies. As usual, Ruby nestled up to Tommy even though the puppies squirmed and scrambled for Ruby's teats. Tommy ignored the puppies and remained only interested in Ruby.

As the weeks passed, the puppies gained size and strength, but Ruby seemed to grow weaker. Victoria thought that Ruby was struggling to provide nutrition for the puppies, so she tried to give her extra food, but it made only a little difference. Victoria reasoned that she would need to rehome the puppies as soon as possible, but the girls had already fallen in love with them and wanted to keep them all. Reluctantly, Victoria agreed that they could keep just one.

After some debate or to be more accurate, an argument in which Shelly threw her cereal over Laura, it was decided that they would keep the little white one. He was different from the other two. The other two looked more like Ruby. The little white one didn't resemble anything Victoria had ever seen.

"What are you going to call him?" Victoria asked. She instantly regretted the question, fearing another fight.

"Fluffy," said Shelly.

Victoria, quick to dispel any further discussion, asked, "Why Fluffy?"

"Because he's fluffy," said Laura, stating a fact.

So Fluffy, it is, thought Victoria was only too pleased that the girls had agreed.

Two days later, Victoria came downstairs late. That morning was unusual because Tommy had slept longer, so they all came down together. As Victoria entered the room, it was obvious something wasn't right. Ruby was led half in and half out of her bed. Her head lulled to the side and her tongue was hanging out. Ruby had passed away in the night. Two of the puppies ignored the scene and played in the corner of the room and Fluffy was still trying to suckle. To Victoria, it looked obscene. Ruby, who had tried so hard to mother the pups, had finally succumbed to the drain on her body. And Fluffy was still demanding one last feed like a final kick to Tommy's friend.

The girls cried for a while, but Victoria told them all the things that children need to know about death. Ruby has gone to heaven to be Jesus's dog. "But why can't Jesus get his own dog?" asked Shelly.

"It's because Ruby is so special," explained Victoria. "And anyway, you've got Fluffy."

After a short time, the girls seemed to accept the situation. With a few sniffs, they packed their school bags and readied themselves for the day ahead.

As they were about to leave the house, Tommy started to scream. It was as if he had just realized that Ruby had gone. He screamed for two solid hours until he fell into an exhausted sleep. Victoria contacted the local dog shelter. They agreed to take two of the puppies and sold Victoria some expensive milk formula and a syringe for Fluffy. Thankfully, Fluffy was already showing interest in solid food, so Victoria was able to wean him within a couple of weeks.

For a while all seemed to go well in Victoria's household. The girls continued to flourish. Becky and her daughter were frequent visitors and they often took the children to the park. Jeff continued to visit but Victoria knew that it was over and there was no chance he would ever come back as too much had passed between them. Now, Victoria felt strong and resentful that Jeff had been too weak to stay and support his family. She still loved him but knew that those deep feelings of being truly joined together were lost.

Tommy seemed to be making good progress in his new nursery. He had learned new words and finally started to call Victoria *mum*. Victoria felt overwhelming love for Tommy, who had been dealt such a cruel blow but was trying and showing real signs of progress. Every time he said mum, she felt a rush of pride and emotion. Each tiny development made Victoria's heart leap. She knew that Tommy would always struggle, but she knew he would always fight. His future was now full of possibilities.

Tommy never seemed to find the comfort with Fluffy that he had with Ruby. Most of the time, there was an indifference between them. But it was still a surprise when Fluffy started to growl at Tommy.

Then, one day, Victoria walked into the room to see Fluffy backed into a corner. Tommy sat in the middle of the floor. They were staring at each other. Fluffy was growling a low, malicious growl. To Victoria's knowledge, Tommy hadn't done anything to provoke Fluffy. Now, they were staring at each other. Fluffy's teeth were bared and Tommy was looking at Fluffy with a loathful look.

Victoria quickly snatched Tommy up and left the room. Fluffy continued to growl until they were out of sight. Victoria felt a sickly feeling. What was happening? She didn't feel that she could trust Fluffy.

Over the next few weeks, the situation seemed to get worse. Fluffy showed no sign of aggression towards the girls but had a complete intolerance of Tommy. Fluffy often growled when Tommy entered the room and Tommy clearly felt the same way. Tommy growled back.

Fluffy was turning into a big dog. At six months, he was already taller than Ruby had been. Victoria tried to remember the dog that she found in the garden with Ruby. *How big was it? What type? Was it actually fluffy?* She couldn't remember. But Fluffy now had a square jaw and bared his teeth in a malicious gesture. He was tall, and Victoria suspected he would easily grow to waist height. Victoria got anxious when she realized he was already as tall as Tommy's face. He was thick-set, too, strong and difficult to control on the lead.

But, sometimes, he looked like one innocent little dog. He seemed to have a sad expression and unusual fur. It was soft to the touch but gleamed in the sunshine. He was a handsome dog. He would look at you with his adorable little puppy eyes full of love until Tommy was out of his sight. The moment Tommy came near him, his puppy eyes would vanish and he'd start growling at him. It hardly seemed like the same dog.

The final straw came when Victoria was holding Tommy on her lap. She wasn't paying much attention as Fluffy growled, which he always did. Victoria was sitting at the kitchen table reading her post and didn't notice that Fluffy had been under the table. He suddenly pounced and bit Tommy's foot. Victoria startled and grabbed Tommy, trying to release him from the snarling beast. Fluffy seemed to lose his grip but still had hold of the bottom of Tommy's trousers. It took all Victoria's strength to drag Tommy away from Fluffy. The moment Fluffy released Tommy, Victoria felt blood dripping off his foot.

At that moment, Victoria knew Fluffy had to go. Victoria spent sleepless nights wondering how to tell the girls. Should she lie and tell them Fluffy had gone and Jesus had another dog? And what about Fluffy? Was he really aggressive? Tommy was different, and he would scream all the time, which must've annoyed Fluffy as he wasn't aggressive with anyone else. So, in all likelihood, Fluffy could be a good family dog with a normal family.

In the end Victoria decided to see if the local rehoming centre would allow her to swap Fluffy for another dog. Something smaller and cuter. Something that would make the girls happy and take away the sting of losing Fluffy.

So after dropping the girls at school and Tommy with Becky, Victoria and Fluffy headed for the rehoming center. "It's highly unethical!" exclaimed the kennel maid. "You can't just swap dogs like you swap playing cards."

"But he's growing so big," explained Victoria. "My little boy is disabled and loves dogs. It would break his heart if he hasn't got a dog but I can't cope with Fluffy. He's so strong."

At the mention of a disabled child, the kennel maid seemed to melt slightly. "Well, I suppose we could break the rules in some cases," she relented. "Particularly because Fluffy will be easy to rehome. He's a handsome dog and we do have a border terrier which may suit you better. He's young but will make a good family dog."

"Yes, that would be great," Victoria said, trying not to sound too eager. At this stage she just wanted to get rid of Fluffy.

"So Fluffy…" said the kennel maid. "You say he's been brought up around children."

"Oh yes," said Victoria. "A real family dog. It's just that he's so strong. He knocks my little boy flying. He just loves playing with Fluffy, but he's big now and still growing." She hoped her blushes wouldn't give her away. She hated telling lies, but the kennel would never take an aggressive dog.

"So what sort of breed is Fluffy?" asked the kennel maid, eying Fluffy curiously.

"I have no clue," said Victoria truthfully. "I know his mother was a spaniel, but goodness knows about the father. He was an intruder into my garden, so the puppies were a complete surprise."

The kennel maid eyed Fluffy. "Well, he's big, so possibly a giant poodle, but his fur is an unusual texture and he's a stocky chap with the strength of a St Bernard."

"Saint Bernards are so sweet-natured," said Victoria, latching on to the idea that Fluffy was some sort of giant teddy.

"Okay!" said the kennel maid with a sigh. "I'll go and fetch Max and we'll take Fluffy."

As Victoria walked away from the rehoming center, Max trotted by her side. He was small and easy on a lead. Victoria actually enjoyed her walk back to Becky's to pick up Tommy.

As she approached Becky's house, she could hear Tommy screaming, but as Becky opened the door, Tommy caught sight of Max and instantly stopped screaming.

"Wuby!" exclaimed Tommy.

A word Victoria thought Tommy had forgotten. Yes, she'd done the right thing. Max was going to fill the gap Ruby had left, and she knew the girls would adore Max.

Peace at last.

CHAPTER 2
JILL'S STORY

Jill wandered down the row of pens at the animal rehoming center.

"I lost my partner a few months ago," explained Jill. "I just want some company. The house feels so empty."

The kennel maid was optimistic and hoped Jill would pick one of the dogs that might be difficult to home. Living alone with no children and working from home made Jill an ideal owner for any dog. Jill owned a house with a garden and earned enough money to feed a large dog and pay any vet bills.

It's obvious this lady has a few bob, thought the kennel maid. Quite apart from the posh car parked outside, she had a presence. She was dressed in casual clothes, navy trousers and a striped top, but the cut made them hang in a certain way. These weren't clothes from the local high street. Her make-up was perfect and blended beautifully and her short blond bob returned instantly to its shape when she shook her head—definitely a professional cut.

Class. Pure class, thought the kennel maid.

The kennel maid thought about Barny. "Barmy! Barny!" as the kennel maids called him, was a very ugly large crossbreed. He had a loud bark and jumped at the kennel bars in excitement. He also did somersaults, which made him completely unsuitable for anyone with less than a hundred-foot square lounge. Either that or the potential owner would need a lot of patience and not many breakable objects. The kennel maid suspected that Jill may have a suitably large lounge or probably a mansion.

Barny was sort of grey. A dirty grey that made him look like he had greasy hair. He also had a huge pair of balls which couldn't be missed or ignored. They seemed to glow like Christmas baubles and forced Barny's back legs apart. Not that Barny was bothered by it and the vet said he wasn't in any discomfort, so he had been allowed to keep his manhood intact. What difference did it make? He was ugly anyway, so if someone was prepared to take the front view, lopsided ears, a protruding tongue, and the greasy-looking beard which refused to lie flat, then what difference was a pair of massive balls going to make?

"I've got an ideal dog for you," said the kennel maid enthusiastically, "Barny is adorable. You'll love him," but the kennel maid realized that she was talking to herself. As she turned, she realized Jill had already stopped by a pen and was staring thoughtfully into the bars.

"Tell me about this one," said Jill thoughtfully.

Sounding less enthusiastic, the kennel maid drawled, "His name is Fluffy. He's only been here a week and I know he'll be easy to home. Great with kids. Some of our other dogs are too stressed to be homed by families and you haven't got children, so it would be great if you could take one of the other dogs."

Jill turned and shot the kennel maid a disgusted look. Jill had had a miscarriage some years ago and had never really gotten over it. Now, to be assessed for a dog on her inability to carry a child seemed abhorrent. What was this stupid young girl talking about? It made Jill more determined. Fluffy looked at Jill with a sad expression and Jill's heart melted. He was an odd-looking dog, but those eyes could melt icebergs. He was handsome but unusual. His pure white coat had a silky sheen that caught the light, but he was soft to the touch and pushed his head up to the bars to be stroked.

"I'll take him," said Jill decisively.

The kennel maid, in an attempt to salvage the situation, explained that if Jill took one of the dogs that had been in kennels for over six months, she could do so with no charge. But taking Fluffy meant that there would be a suggested donation of £100. The kennel maid was tempted to double the fee in an effort to persuade Jill, but Jill was focused and didn't want to look any further. She had made up her mind. It was Fluffy or nothing.

With a sigh, the kennel maid said, "Okay, I'll do the paperwork."

Poor Barny was left barking with excitement in the bottom pen. "Perhaps next time Barny," muttered the kennel maid under her breath.

Jill completed the adoption form. It was a lengthy form, which Jill found frustrating. "Why do they want so many details?" she was asked if she had owned a dog before, did she had an enclosed garden and would the dog had been left alone for periods of more than an hour. Then the form asked about her income, visitors to the family home and any other pets. She passed the form back to the kennel maid.

The kennel maid read the form with a frown on her face. "Sorry…" said the kennel maid. "But you don't really meet the adoption criteria."

"What do you mean?" asked Jill sharply.

"I just work here," said the kennel maid. "But I have instructions to say I should only let dogs go to people who are likely to be able to control and contain them. You haven't had a dog before and your garden isn't fully fenced. The dog could easily get out and run riot. Fluffy is a big dog and could be a huge problem if he is out of control."

Jill didn't move. She felt dismayed, irritated and angry, and an angry Jill could cut through the ice as if it were peanut butter.

"My garden…" Jill sighed. "Is over an acre of land, with an area at the bottom which has been left unattended, ideal for a dog. I work at home, so the dog would rarely, if ever, be left unattended. I'm not sure who you think would be better placed to house one of your dogs. Do you actually want to find homes for these dogs? Perhaps you think a council flat where the dog can be locked in all day would be better."

The kennel maid eyed Jill, thinking that she did have a point. "Can you fence the garden?" asked the kennel maid. "Perhaps if you sign a form declaring that you intend to fence the garden…"

But Jill wasn't a lady used to giving in. For many years, Jill had negotiated contracts for her business. She could read people and used this skill to manipulate and intimidate them. She could see the kennel maid wasn't an educated girl. Jill took a step forward, emphasizing her height and towering over the young girl. She came forward and replied with a calm tone, "I can make a substantial donation and write a letter to the owners to tell them how helpful you have been.

Or, of course, I could write a letter to say how unhelpful you've been." She smiled a sinister smile and watched as the kennel maid shrank like a popped balloon. She had no words left and was struggling to meet Jill's gaze.

Jill glanced down at the form. The proprietor, Mr. B. Owen, was listed in small print at the top of the form. "Mr. Owen is the owner," I believe. "The same Mr. Owen who attended my dinner party last month." Jill was bluffing but she guessed the kennel maid would have no idea of Mr Owen's lifestyle or personal life.

"You know him?" asked the kennel maid, looking up.

"I know a lot of people," Jill replied. "A lot of important people."

"Well, I suppose it will be okay then. I'm sorry, but we do have to be careful," said the kennel maid. Some of our dogs have been returned when they have been recaptured, roaming the streets. All dogs in our care are likely to exhibit challenging behavior after being abandoned and shut in kennels. Fluffy is a big dog and is likely to get bigger. He may take a bit of handling. We haven't had time to assess him, so we've got no idea if he chases cats or even if he pulls on a lead."

"If I have issues, I'll hire a dog trainer," said Jill. "The dog will stand a much better chance with me."

The kennel maid knew this was probably true. Rules are meant to be broken and Mr Owen would surely be pleased with a substantial donation. Fluffy was snuggled up to Jill's leg. "Sometimes dogs pick their own owners," said the kennel maid, smiling at Fluffy.

It took a few minutes as the kennel maid entered the details into the computer, ticking the box that said the garden was enclosed and the dog wouldn't be left alone.

As Jill left the kennel maid had a brief thought that she should have checked with Mr. Owen, but it was too late now.

If Mr. Owen did know Jill, he probably wouldn't be pleased to be disturbed by a telephone call. If he didn't, she would be told off for being gullible. Either way, the phone call was probably a bad idea. She turned the cheque over, which Jill had left next to her computer and gasped. *Three thousand pounds!* Mr. Owen would be pleased, of that she was sure. She watched Jill disappear into the car park, then turned to try to comfort poor Barny, who sounded louder than ever.

Jill put Fluffy in her new dog carrier at the back of her Landrover Discovery. Jill recalled the day she bought the car. It was a present to herself after she lost Brian. She could afford it and thought she would enjoy going out for drives in the countryside. But without Brian, nothing seemed enjoyable. She woke every morning to the emptiness in her house and the physical pain of the loss in her stomach.

"And now I'm trying to replace you with a dog."

A Protected Killer

She still spoke to Brian as if he were there and prayed for some sort of answer or sign that he still existed somewhere or somehow. She missed Brian every second of every day. There was no relief to the pain Jill felt. The pain took her by surprise. She had heard people say about a loss causing physical pain, but she hadn't thought it possible before she lost Brian. The pain came on suddenly and without warning. She found it difficult to go out; when she was forced to join any social gathering. She often had to run to the ladies' room to lock herself in and cry. Jill knew she needed something more in her life. She had very few friends. Only Brian had been her friend. And now people didn't seem to know what to say, so they avoided being around her. She had a strained relationship with her parents. Work had taken a lot of her time and Brian had taken the rest. She was too busy to visit her parents often, so they drifted apart.

Jill had never told her parents about her pregnancy and miscarriage. She felt it was something between Brian and herself. They used to comfort each other, cry, and hug each other. It was their shared grief and Jill didn't want to share it with anyone else. But now she had no one. She had not only lost her baby but also her soul mate.

When she phoned her parents to tell them Brian had been killed in a car accident, her mother had said, "Oh dear. Will you expect us to come to the funeral?"

Jill had told them they didn't need to come. It would be a small and quick affair, so they didn't need to travel the thirty miles to attend. Jill hadn't really expected anything different but still felt hurt that they hadn't offered to support her.

Brian's parents had never really liked Jill. Brian, in his excitement, had told them about the baby, but when Jill miscarried, they had made it clear that they believed it was because Jill had put her work over the welfare of her unborn child.

The miscarriage was unexplained, "Just one of those things," the doctor had said. "Try again." But although Jill never took contraception, she never conceived again—*just one of those things.*

Now, at forty-five and without a partner, she knew she could not have children. She was alone in life and likely to stay that way.

She was a practical woman and had vowed she wouldn't start referring to the dog as her baby and her as his mummy. But when she looked at those sorrowful eyes in her driving mirror, she knew that a lot of her rules were going to be broken.

Fluffy had instantly stolen her heart.

"Fluffy!" she said to herself and smiled to herself. "Who on earth calls a lolloping great mutt like you, Fluffy? I'll have to change it. I know you've got used to Fluffy, but we could try Duffy or Tufty because you've got a bit of a tuft on your head. But Tufty sounds nearly as bad as Fluffy." She spent the rest of the drive home thinking of words that rhymed with Fluffy. When she'd run out of English words, she tried to think of French, Spanish or German words. Jill was fluent in all three languages and spoke a bit of Italian and Polish.

Many years ago she had set up a business selling specialist catering equipment. Through hard work the business had expanded and now had outlets across Europe. Jill had traveled extensively in the early years, but now the business was established and she was able to work at home and employ a management team to do the running around.

Brian also had a business and worked in IT developing softward. They had a wonderful life and perhaps with the exception of a child, they wanted for nothing. They used to spend days together using the same room in the house as a joint office. They liked the closeness, never tired of each other's company, and shared everything. They used to go on holidays to exotic, remote islands and places where they could be alone together. They'd spend evenings in front of the TV, sipping wine in each other's arms and would make love. Real love. Not sex. When they made love, Jill felt the closeness of Brian—the joining of not just their bodies but their very being.

Everything about Brian made Jill happy. She loved his smile, the way he yawned at the end of a TV program, the way he touched her face and the piece of his hair which refused to lie flat.

Of course, there were issues when she lost a big contract and Brian broke his leg climbing over the fence. They would always catch the flu at the same time. Brian's mother visited briefly and there would always be an argument, but nothing mattered. Being in love with Brian was everything. They were untouchable. And with him, there was really no such thing as a bad day.

Then, one night, everything was destroyed when she saw the policeman at the door. Brian had gone out to fetch a bottle of wine for them to share. He had only been gone for half an hour. She didn't cry. Somehow, she held it together for the sake of the policemen who had to give her the news. But once they left, she fell to the floor and wept until every drop of fluid in her body had turned to tears.

The following weeks were a blur. Funeral arrangements, papers to sign, solicitors to see. People commented on how well she was coping, but Jill felt numb. She couldn't believe she was alone. She tried to cook meals Brian would like, trying to gain some normality as if he would walk back in. But then she would throw the meals in the bin, along with her tear-soaked tissues.

She often thought she wanted to end her life. But she knew Brian would want her to go on. She continually listened for a sound or any sort of sign that he still existed.

She kept Brian's toothbrush next to hers in the bathroom. And every night, she cuddled up to his pillow and tried to breathe in the fading scent of his hair.

The idea of a dog was impulsive and sudden. She couldn't stand the emptiness in the house. She quite liked dogs. The thought of another being in the house might help fill the horrid, empty silence. It felt like a last attempt at life.

It was getting dark as Jill pulled into her drive. Her house was large and modern. The security lights came on and she used her remote control to open her garage door without getting out of the car. Once the garage door was closed she opened the car and the internal door into the utility room. Brian had been keen on security and had designed the entry to the house so that she didn't have to leave the car until the exterior was secure.

Fluffy jumped out without hesitation. He wandered through the utility room, kitchen, and into the lounge. It was only then he stopped to sniff around. He examined each chair and selected the one closest to the radiator. He jumped on the chair and nestled down. Jill had bought an expensive dog bed, but Fluffy looked comfortable, so she left him where he was.

"Perhaps just tonight," she told him. "Want something to eat, Fluffy?"

Fluffy seemed to understand and followed Jill into the kitchen. Jill had purchased the most expensive dog food and had a cupboard full of it. She didn't want her special new friend to put up with tacky, cheap food. She scooped the food out into the new dog bowl and proudly presented it to Fluffy. Fluffy sniffed, then wandered over to the other side of the kitchen where Jill had put two pieces of cooked chicken breasts to make herself a sandwich. Fluffy sat gazing up at the worktop expectantly.

Jill laughed. "Okay, perhaps this once."

Jill suddenly realized that she had laughed. She couldn't remember laughing since Brian died. She felt guilty but Fluffy wagged his tail and seemed to smile at her. Fluffy was welcome to the chicken. In the short time he had been in her house he had lifted her spirit. She would get herself some toast.

When they returned to the living room, Fluffy jumped into the chair and Jill sat on the sofa. Fluffy seemed to think about this, then jumped down from the chair and onto the sofa, where he laid across Jill's lap as if he'd been there forever.

They stayed there all evening until Jill's eyes started to droop. She took Fluffy into the garden for a pee, then returned to the living room. She had planned to put Fluffy in the kitchen in his new bed, but he jumped back onto the sofa as if he wanted her to join him.

"Okay," said Jill. "You win. You can stay there just for tonight." Jill turned off the light. "Good night, Fluffy."

But before Jill was halfway up the stairs, Fluffy jumped at the door, pushed the handle down and was at the top of the stairs before Jill. He hardly hesitated. Although there were four bedrooms, Fluffy sniffed the air and seemed to know which bedroom was Jill's. By the time Jill had reached the landing Fluffy was on Jill's bed.

That broke all the rules. Jill did not want to share her bed with a dog. But it was a big bed and it was Fluffy's first night. So perhaps just this once.

In the following weeks, Jill became increasingly attached to Fluffy and broke all the rules she had set before Fluffy's arrival. Fluffy's diet consisted partially of very expensive dog food and partially of treats. Accept that treats are something you would expect occasionally. Fluffy had treats every day. Sometimes cooked chicken, salmon and even biscuits with caviar. He spent every evening cuddled up to Jill on her sofa and every night cuddled up to Jill on her bed. She brushed his soft coat and it gleamed. He was gentle and took food from her hand, never allowing his teeth to come into contact with her skin. He was obedient. He would sit and stay on command and seemed to know everything Jill said. If Jill cried, Fluffy would nestle closer to her. It was as if he knew her sorrow and tried to comfort her.

She still spoke to Brian. But Fluffy seemed to understand and often stared at Brian's photograph. Jill found this comforting. Fluffy seemed to be connecting with Brian. Maybe there were three of them in the house.

The weeks rolled into months and then into a full year. Jill fell in love with Fluffy. Jill had tried to get him to answer to Duffy, Buffy, and even You Adorable Doggy Doos, but he would only really respond to Fluffy, so Jill gave in. Fluffy it was. Jill had a large back garden mostly laid to lawn and overlooking fields. A gardener came once a week to mow the lawns, but Fluffy didn't bother to go out when he was there.

It was just Fluffy and Jill and Jill didn't mind one bit. She still missed Brian, but Fluffy filled the house with new joy. Fluffy's toys were everywhere. Fluffy was everywhere. Fluffy could open doors, so he followed Jill when she went for a shower, sitting outside the shower cubicle until she emerged. Fluffy sat with Jill on the sofa and went to bed with her at night. When Jill worked on her computer in the daytime, Fluffy would sit quietly at her feet.

As the weather got warmer and the back door was open, Fluffy would sometimes lie outside. He always went to the toilet at the bottom of the garden, never in the middle of the lawn. Sometimes, Fluffy would sneak into the field behind the garden, but he never wandered far and would always come when called, so it was never a problem.

A Protected Killer

Never, that was until that fateful day when Fluffy returned from the garden with strange marks on his white fur. Jill hadn't noticed him missing. It was a warm day so Fluffy had gone outside to lie down. He usually lay where Jill could see him. She thought she remembered glancing up once or twice and seeing him there but was absorbed in her work and hadn't paid much attention. He'd been out there for about half an hour on his own. There was nothing unusual. It had started to get chilly, so Jill called him in and closed the door.

It wasn't until they were watching TV that evening that Jill noticed. She had been stroking Fluffy when she realised that her hand was covered in something sticky. It was a browny-red color. Her first thought was that she'd touched something, so with a degree of annoyance, she got up to wash her hands. But then she saw that the substance, whatever it was, was around Fluffy's head, mouth and chest. Fluffy's thick fur had hidden most of it. The weather had turned the sky into a dark mass of clouds, so the room had been in semi-darkness, which was why Jill hadn't noticed it earlier. Fluffy had probably tried to wash himself so the substance wasn't visible on the surface of Fluffy's coat. But as she parted Fluffy's fur, she could see that Fluffy was smothered in the gooey substance.

"What on earth have you been doing, Fluffy?" asked Jill as if expecting an answer. "You've been rolling onto something?"

Fluffy looked at Jill with his sad eyes.

"Oh, come on," she said. "Now I've got to get you cleaned up in the shower."

Fluffy hated showers. He could look really sorry for himself in a shower, but he was obedient and sat quietly while Jill sprayed him with warm water and shampooed his white fur. After a shower Fluffy was even more beautiful. His white fur seemed to shimmer and the soft patches were so soft Jill wanted to nestle into him and stay there touching his warm, fresh-smelling, softness.

As she rubbed the shampoo into his fur, she thought that the substance could be blood. She checked Fluffy for any cuts or injuries. There were none. "Dogs will be dogs!" she told herself. "If there's something messy, they'll roll in it."

She felt a slight concern that it could be a substance used by a farmer on the field, but the field had been left wild for years, so unless Fluffy had wandered some distance, it was unlikely. And Fluffy didn't wander far. On the rare occasions that he'd gone out of sight, she'd called him only to find that he'd been right there, just behind the wheelbarrow or the compost heap. He did wander into the field occasionally, but only on the other side of the fence, still visible from the house.

Just one of those things, she thought. *I'll probably never know what you've been up to, Fluffy.*

They spent the evening together as usual on the sofa and fell asleep during the evening news. As the theme tune played, Jill headed for bed. Fluffy, as always, bounded ahead of Jill and onto the bed. As Jill climbed into bed, she knew that while she would never get over losing Brian, Fluffy had improved her life. She thought that Brian had sent Fluffy to her to give her comfort and companionship. As she looked at Brian's photograph, she wished him goodnight and told him she loved him as she always did. But that night, she thanked Brian for sending Fluffy.

"We're sharing Fluffy' she told him.

Fluffy nestled into her and she could smell the sweet shampoo. He was soft and warm. She put her arm across him and saw that his eyes were closed. He was breathing softly, sound asleep and totally content. She felt her eyelids getting heavy; before long, she had fallen into a deep, dreamless sleep.

The next morning, Jill woke to the sound of the birds singing. She jumped out of bed with a spring in her step, went downstairs and opened the door for Fluffy to go out for his morning pee. Jill put the kettle on and made herself some toast. Then she sat at her computer and turned on one of the news sites as she always did. Suddenly she froze with the toast in her mouth and her brain started reading the headline which says: "Child attacked by a vicious dog". Then underneath, "police are still hunting for the dog which remains at large. Child detained in hospital with horrific injuries."

There was a picture which she recognized instantly. It was the row of houses that backed onto the small wood, which backed onto the field at the bottom of her garden. She didn't read anymore. Feeling sick, she ran to the back door shouting Fluffy.

Fluffy appeared as he always did when she called him. He looked at her with his sad eyes. She bent and put her arms around him. Her stomach churned as she thought of the substance on Fluffy's fur. A mixture of emotions overtook her—fear, suspicion and an overwhelming desire to protect her friend. Surely, this had to be wrong. *Not Fluffy. It couldn't be Fluffy.* But she didn't want Fluffy anywhere near the backfield. She would keep Fluffy with her until the dangerous dog was caught. Fluffy could be mistaken for the vicious dog. She needed to keep him where she could see him.

Not Fluffy. Not Fluffy. It can't be Fluffy. That wasn't blood.

Later that morning, Jill paced around her living room, trying to think. She'd read every article about the dog attack and watched the news on every channel.

She'd established that the child lived about five minutes away from her house. On the far side of the field, at the back of Jill's house, was a small wooded area and the child's house was behind that. Fluffy, to Jill's knowledge, had never wandered that far. Fluffy had never gone out of sight of the house.

The child was attacked at about three in the afternoon. Fluffy was in the garden at about three in the afternoon. Or at least Jill thought Fluffy was in the garden. Had she checked? Had she glanced out of the window and seen Fluffy in the garden? Sometimes, she felt sure she had. Sometimes, she hadn't.

Fluffy watched Jill pacing around from his position on the sofa, scared to believe that Fluffy attacked the kid child. He looked beautiful. So docile, so loving, so sad. Jill had never seen any aggression in Fluffy. But Fluffy didn't see many people and certainly no children. Could Jill be sure he wasn't aggressive? Sadly, she realised the only thing she could say with certainty was that Fluffy wasn't aggressive towards her.

It was reported that the child had been playing in her back garden. The garden backed onto the trees. The mother heard the scream and ran to the back door. She had seen the dog disappearing into the trees. She hadn't got a good look at the dog because the scene when she reached the back door was so horrific. She hadn't concentrated on the dog so had only seen it's white tail. The child, just three and a half, had her arm hanging off. The emergency services guessed that the dog had grabbed the child by the arm and shook her so hard that it ripped her arm away from her body. Although the emergency services were called immediately, the child had lost so much blood that she was now in intensive care, fighting for her life.

This could not be Fluffy. Surely, this could not be Fluffy. Thoughts rushed into Jill's head. What sort of mother leaves her three-year-old in the garden? Three-year-olds often grab animals and are cruel to them. Perhaps this three-year-old had tormented the dog.

Then, other thoughts, there could be no excuse. A dog capable of that sort of behaviour has to be destroyed. Then she looked at Fluffy. No, it couldn't be Fluffy. It wasn't Fluffy. But Fluffy could be under suspicion.

Jill checked the throw on the sofa for any signs of the sticky substance from Fluffy's coat. She couldn't find any but changed all the throws anyway. She put the used throws in the washing machine along with Fluffy's towels and bath mats. Anything that could have a trace of the substance on it was washed on a boil wash.

I'm being stupid, Jill thought. *It just wasn't Fluffy.* But however many times Jill told herself it wasn't, she couldn't stop the sick feeling in her stomach.

What could she do? What should she do? The textbook answer would be to admit her suspicions to the police. They would investigate and Fluffy would be in the clear.

But perhaps not. They were desperate to catch the dog and by offering Fluffy up as a potential culprit, it would be a gift. They could just say it was the dog. They'd win. They'd caught the dog and destroyed it in record time. Would they even bother to find out if it was the right dog?

No, she wasn't going to turn Fluffy in. Not unless she was sure. And would she ever be sure? But she would never let Fluffy out alone ever again. From now on, if Fluffy needed a pee, Jill would be with him even in her own garden.

Jill spent a disturbed night. Most of the time, she was awake. Was that blood on Fluffy's coat? Perhaps not. It was a brownish colour. But does blood go that colour as it dries? The girl was attacked at around three in the afternoon. She found the substance on Fluffy at around six when they sat curled up on the sofa together to watch TV. And it was still wet. It surely would have dried by then. But she couldn't think what else the substance could be. And it wouldn't take long for Fluffy to reach the trees and the houses on the other side.

Okay, what if it was blood? Fluffy could have killed a rabbit. She had seen rabbits in the field. When she slept, it was a mixture of wild thoughts of Brian being bitten by Fluffy, then Brian being arrested and taken away, and even Fluffy being bitten by Brian.

At five in the morning, Jill had enough and got up. She made herself a strong coffee. Fluffy sensed something was wrong and nestled up to Jill's leg affectionately.

"It's okay, Fluffy. I know you love me and I know you wouldn't hurt anyone. We'll protect each other, no matter what."

Jill hovered over the computer. She usually caught up with the news in the morning. But this morning, she wasn't sure she needed a dose of morning news.

Finally, in a quick flurry of movement, she sighed and turned on the machine. As she clicked on the news headlines, her heart sank as she read. *Toddler loses her fight following a vicious dog attack. The little girl had lost too much blood. Despite the best efforts of emergency staff, the fragile body of the tiny three-and-a-half-year-old had given up.*

She was dead.

Jill spent the next two days in a daze. She watched Fluffy continually, even taking Fluffy to the toilet with her. When Fluffy decided to lie under the table, Jill felt complete panic because she'd lost sight of him for two seconds. Fluffy was used to attention and didn't seem bothered about this new level of care. But he did seem to sense a change and nestled close to Jill, more loving than ever.

"Are you trying to say sorry," Jill whispered to him.

Jill's mind separated her life into compartments. There was her childhood, happy, normal. A bit of strain with her parents, but nothing exceptionable. Then, there was her time with Brian. They'd met while at University on a camping trip to Dorset. She remembered the young Brian sitting by the campfire, the fire turning Brian's handsome face into a warm orange glow. She couldn't remember what they'd talked about or how they had got together. But she remembered sitting close to him. She remembered feeling like there was no one else there. She remembered their love, which lasted solid and strong throughout their marriage.

The next compartment was bringing Fluffy home. Feeling the instant connection. Laughing for the first time since Brian had died. Finally, feeling like she may be able to build some sort of life.

And now a new chapter. Was this called *Life after Fluffy had killed?* Confusion, dismay, fear. Her life felt as if it had suddenly been turned upside down – again. She couldn't dismiss the thoughts and couldn't completely convince herself that Fluffy was not a vicious murderer. She couldn't, try as she might feel the way she felt before the attack. That's how she referred to it. An attack. Not an accident. An attack. Whatever had happened, it wasn't an accident.

She could hardly bring herself to read the news reports, but she read every one. Sometimes, turning away with tears in her eyes. Trying to convince herself that she was wrong and that she should pull herself together and get back to her life.

Somehow, her mind started counting the days since the attack. Unable to eat or sleep properly, she couldn't concentrate on work. She wandered through the house, not even able to recall what day it was. She remembered a feeling very similar to this when she had lost Brian. But Fluffy was a dog. How could she compare losing her wonderful husband to the behaviour of a dog?

Night passed and the sun came, but Jill could hardly sleep—choked on toast—lots of coffee—night terrors. She tried sleeping on the sofa and dozed off on the bed. And every time she closed her eyes, she woke in a panic. "Where's Fluffy?" And he was right next to her, trying to comfort her while nuzzling her hand, unable to understand that he was responsible for the panic.

There were more news reports giving graphic details of the child's injuries. Arm ripped off, broken ribs, bite marks to the face. *Vicious beast. Must be caught. Must be destroyed. People shouldn't keep animals unless they can control them.* Dog wardens were on patrol, catching any dog that put its nose out of a garden gate. Mothers were interviewed, saying they would cross the road rather than walk past a dog.

More night terrors. More toast. More coffee. Emptying the contents of her stomach into the toilet. Mascara smeared down her cheek. Had she even put make-up on? She couldn't remember. More news reports. More horror.

Then, a knock on the door. What day was it? How many days since the attack? It made Jill jump. She carefully shut Fluffy in the kitchen and edged towards the front door. She opened it just wide enough to peer out. Two police officers stood on the doorstep. Her heart was beating so hard that she thought it would be seen through her tee shirt.

"Yes," said Jill, trying to keep her voice level and calm

"Sorry to bother you," said the young policewoman. "We're just carrying out house-to-house inquiries relating to the dog attack. It's actually a short distance, as the crow flies, across the field, so we were wondering if you could help."

"I don't have a dog," Jill uttered the words swiftly.

"No, but perhaps you saw a dog wandering around. We have reports that the dog disappeared into the trees, so it could have been heading in this direction."

"Sorry," said Jill. "No, I'm mostly engrossed in my work, so I haven't got time to stare out of the window."

Jill thought about her appearance. Could her tear-stained face give her away? Would they know something was wrong? She added quickly, "I've had flu, so I've been in bed... didn't even get the time to check the news."

"Sorry to hear that," said the police officer in a matter-of-fact voice. "And do you live alone? Is there someone else we can talk to?"

"No," said Jill. "I live alone."

"Okay, well, if you think of anything or if you see a stray dog, can you call us immediately?" said the police officer while passing a card through the gap in the door.

"I will," said Jill, attempting a smile.

She closed the door quickly. *Too quickly,* she thought. She slid down the wall into a sitting position. Her heart was pounding and she was shaking. Why had she lied to the police? Why didn't she let them in? They could have seen what a beautiful placid animal Fluffy is. And they would have just gone away, dismissing Fluffy from their thoughts. But the reason she lied crept upon her like a black smothering fog. The reason was that deep inside her. She knew.

Another restless night. The police would be back. Her behaviour, despite her excuses, had definitely been odd. She had peered through a gap in the door and sounded abrupt and unwelcoming. Surely, the police would see she was hiding something.

Jill led a fairly reclusive life. Her work meant she rarely had visitors to the house. Meetings were conducted remotely by computer and she had no one she would call a friend. The nearest house was some distance down the road.

Occasionally, she had been involved in local projects. It was obvious Jill wasn't short of money, so when the church steeple was in need of repair, the church committee knocked on Jill's door, She had contributed generously and been invited to a thank-you lunch. She didn't much like these sorts of events, but this was in the daytime, so she attended and left Fluffy in the car for an hour, checking him constantly. But no one had talked about her dog. Did they know she had one?

Fluffy liked a car ride. And he was always well behaved, so there didn't seem much point in leaving him at home. As long as the weather wasn't too hot, Jill would take him on trips to the supermarket or car refuel.

People knew Jill to pass the time of day. Although they weren't friends, she had acquaintances, most of whom had seen Fluffy in the car. Then there was the gardener, the postman, the delivery driver, all of whom had seen Fluffy occasionally and knew she owned a dog.

But she had lied to the police. Surely, she would be found out, and it would bring more suspicion. She shouldn't have lied. Or should she? She still wanted to believe that it wasn't Fluffy, but it was becoming increasingly difficult. Even if it was Fluffy, he must have been provoked. Perhaps the child hurt him, grabbed him and wouldn't let go. They said the dog ran into the woods. Perhaps Fluffy had been frightened.

By four in the morning, she was convinced that it was just a matter of time before the police would come for Fluffy and he would be destroyed. Humanely destroyed, they say. But is destroying a beautiful animal humane?

Fluffy slept peacefully beside her. To admit to the police that she had lied would be passing a death sentence to Fluffy. It was just before five when she had an idea. She could save

Fluffy. Although not ideal, all she needed was a place where Fluffy would be watched continually. A place where he would never be left unsupervised, and a place far from here where he could never be associated with this area. If the police came again, she would tell them she used to have a dog, but he had died a few months ago. It was the best thing she could do for her friend. She could give him another chance.

She rose quickly and made a strong coffee. She picked up all of Fluffy's toys and brushes, putting them into a black bag. His food and feeding bowl went into another bag. She checked around the house. Not a sign of a dog. Okay, there were probably hairs, but if she had owned a dog previously, the presence of hairs wouldn't be suspicious. Then she took a bottle of wine from the fridge and headed for the car with Fluffy at her side.

She reached the outskirts of London at rush hour and crawled through the traffic. *Good. Hiding in plain sight.* People don't notice people in a crowd, even a dog wasn't that unusual. In London, people can be invisible and so can dogs. People dress in strange clothes and do strange things. London—full of the invisible.

She found a parking space where she could stay for three hours for the price of a second mortgage, but that was no problem. At least it was an old-style pay and display, meaning there would be no record of her car being there. She was sure that it could be traced if anyone looked. But they would be unlikely to look and if nothing showed obviously on her bank statements, the chances were her short detour into London City would go unnoticed. It was unlikely that anyone would ever look, but she wanted to do this properly. No trace, no way of tracking Fluffy down. She spotted him immediately, A huddled shape in a shop doorway. Could this be the one? Plenty more to try if this doesn't work out. She approached the bundle and allowed Fluffy to sniff at the shape.

A young man, dirty with a dark, unshaven face, appeared from under the cover. "Gerroff," he waved Fluffy away. *But not too aggressively,* Jill thought.

Fluffy stood his ground, curious of the smelly shape.

"I said Gerroff," he waved his arm at Fluffy again.

"He likes you," said Jill, smiling

"He'd better not piss on me. They usually try to piss on me."

Jill offered the shape of a five-pound note. He looked at her now through dark-slitted eyes. Suspicious, but taking the five-pound note.

"What's your name?" Jill asked.

"What's it to do with you," replied the smelly shape.

Jill was dressed in her jeans and tee shirt, but even in this attire, she still looked like she had money. The quality of even these casual clothes was obvious.

"I'm Jill," she told the shape. "I can't go home. I need help."

The shape looked at her. "Well, don't look at me. I can't even help myself."

Undeterred, Jill sat on the floor next to him. "I can't go home," she said the same words again. "I'll just sit here."

"Suit yourself," said the shape.

There was a long silence. Fluffy sat between them but eventually turned to the shape and licked his hand.

"Nice dog," said the shape.

"Fluffy," said Jill. "He's wonderful."

"Fluffy?" exclaimed the man. "Who even calls a dog like that? Fluffy!" He laughed a gravelly sound and his face crumpled into a broad smile, exposing a mixture of broken teeth and gums. Jill turned her head away as the putrid smell of the shape's breath reached her nostrils. Fluffy didn't mind, though and seemed to enjoy the smell. He wagged his tail and snuggled between the shape and Jill. Slowly, the man pulled his hand from under the covers, exposing a dirty hip flask. He took a sip and offered it to Jill. She took the flask and took a gulp. She almost choked as the fiery liquid hit her throat.

"My name's Chris," he offered

"Hi Chris," said Jill. "I'm in deep shit."

Chris turned. "Ain't we all? But the difference is, you can go home and sort your shit. I just sit here and live in mine."

"I can't go home," Jill stated flatly.

They sat together without speaking for half an hour. Fluffy, curious about his new companion, licked Chris and nestled up to him.

"Tell you what," Jill said suddenly. "I've got a proposition for you. I can't tell you about my shit, but we might be able to help each other. Fluffy likes you. What if I give you a thousand pounds in cash right now and you look after Fluffy for me."

"Are you for real?" Chris turned to her in disbelief. "A fucking grand to take your dog. Why? For how long?"

"No questions," stated Jill. "A thousand pounds. Cash. But I'll be gone a while. I've got a week's supply of food in this bag. Afterwards, it's up to you. But he's a good friend and he'll keep you warm. I need to go somewhere and he can't come."

Chris looked at her thoughtfully. He looked as if he might refuse, so Jill pulled the bundle of cash from her bulging jeans pocket.

"A thousand pounds," she stated. "But you have to look after him."

"Fucking hell, lady. You must be in deep shit."

He took the money eagerly and Fluffy's lead with a little less enthusiasm. "Well, it looks like we have a deal," he looked at Fluffy with a toothy smile. "Fluffy," he said. Then repeated, "Fluffy."

Jill could hear him laughing as she walked away with tears in her eyes. She didn't look back. She drove out of London and turned onto the road heading for Dorset. She had told Chris the truth when she said she couldn't go home. She had tried so hard to live there without Brian. But she knew now that she couldn't be there without him. The time she had spent with Fluffy felt like a lie. A lie to herself that she could cope without Brian and find some sort of happiness. She missed Brian more than ever now. He had always supported her when things went wrong. She stopped for just long enough to fill up with fuel and dispose of Fluffy's toys in a bin.

After a few hours, she arrived at the cliff top where Brian and she had camped and met all those years ago. She opened the wine and took a large swig. Then another. She sat enjoying the sun on her face and the sweet taste of the wine. Her head felt fuzzy and warm. She sang the song that had played on the radio that warm night all those years ago. She smiled to herself.

Then she opened the fuel cap on the car and started the engine. "I'm coming to be with you, Brian," she whispered.

She put the car into gear and floored the accclerator. The car sailed over the cliff. It bounced twice, then exploded. When the emergency services found the body, it was barely recognisable as a woman.

A week later a newspaper carried a tiny story at the bottom of page four saying that a successful businesswoman had committed suicide following the death of her husband. The main headline read *Hunt for killer dog continues.*

CHAPTER 3
CHRIS'S STORY

Fluffy nestled close to Chris. He felt warm and soft. Chris put his head on Fluffy's neck. *Good pillow, if nothing else,* he thought.

It was probably a bad idea to take in a dog. He hadn't lied to the lady when he said he could barely take care of himself. Chris couldn't remember the last time he had slept in a bed. Once, he had a wife, children and a job—his happy days.

His wife left him for another man because of alcoholism. He'd always been an addict and he prioritized it without caring about anything else.

His wife had an affair with his next-door neighbour. She had told the children that their father was useless. His young children, who were easily influenced, repeated what their mother said. They all told him he was useless.

He struggled to keep his patience as his wife hopped over the fence and into bed with Richard the prick. He got angry. His timekeeping became unimportant and he lost his job. More accusations of uselessness, but the fact that he had lost his job seemed proof. Yes, he was useless. He *felt* useless.

Then one day when he watched his wife disappearing into next door's garden, leaving him to mind the children, he lost it completely. He ran after her and grabbed her by the throat.

Someone called the police and he was taken to police cells where he spent the night. He was then informed that his wife had taken out an injunction order which banned him from going within five miles of the property. He had nowhere to go, a few pounds in his pocket and a half bottle of rum.

He hitchhiked to London. He'd heard homeless people did okay there. He began begging on the street. At first, he thought he would get his life back together. He spent a few nights at a homeless shelter. But when he turned up smelling of drink, they refused to let him in so he stopped trying.

These days he spent the mornings collecting his daily allowance from the Job Centre and the rest of the day with his friends under a bridge. The evenings were for begging. On a good day he could afford a big bottle. On a bad day a small bottle would do. A local charity gave him hot soup and a roll and sometimes a pie or a sandwich. Occasionally someone would buy him a burger. He didn't think about the future. It was all about now. He lived in the moment. But now he had a dog. Of course, he wouldn't keep it. He would dump it as soon as the food ran out. But for now, Fluffy was providing him with warmth and a comfort he hadn't experienced for quite a while. He eyed the dog and it looked back at him. Then something happened that caused Chris to rethink.

"Oh he's gorgeous," said the young blond haired woman as she bent to stroke Fluffy.

"He's all I've got," said Chris. Of course, it was the truth but Chris wasn't going to pass up an opportunity to pull on someone's heart strings.

"He's not well. He need's pills. I'm hoping I can get enough money to pick up his pills."

"How much are the pills?" asked the woman.

"For the whole course it's fifty quid. But if you could spare anything to help, I'd be grateful."

Without any hesitation the woman reached into her handbag and thrust some notes into Chris's hand. *The whole fifty quid.* Chris could hardly believe it. As Chris sat in the doorway Fluffy seemed to draw in all the passers-by. He seemed to have a way of looking completely pathetic. He was affectionate when anyone showed him attention. In fact, Chris broke his usual routine to stay in the doorway rather than going to the bridge to meet the other homeless folk. At the end of the day Chris had just short of three hundred pounds in his pocket. Even when he was working, he hadn't had so much money to spend.

Chris headed for the off licence and bought a bottle of his favorite whisky. Not the cheap stuff. Real whisky. Then he went back to his doorway. A charity worker brought him some soup and someone brought him a burger. He fed Fluffy and gulped the whisky. Then he laid down. He couldn't remember the last time he'd had a day like this. A full belly, a bottle of whisky and the warmth and softness of this animal next to him.

Fluffy seemed to snuggle right into Chris' soul. Perhaps he might keep this dog. Fluffy was all Chris really had and

Fluffy seemed to care about him. No one had shown Chris any care or affection for a very long time.

"Yes mate," said Chris in a drunken drawl. "I reckon you can stay. Still don't like that stupid fucking name though."

Chris fell asleep to the sound of Fluffy's regular breathing and warm breath on his face.

In the following months Fluffy turned Chris' life around. As the notes fell into Chris' upturned hat Chris found he gained status with the other homeless folks in his area. Chris felt like a king. He had enough now to be able to share his food and drink. He even bought another coat from a charity shop.

If business was a bit slow, Chris propped up a notice 'Fluffy needs medicine. Please help!' People would feel pity for Fluffy and drop him a few pounds. It made his day to be able to afford expensive whiskey and good food.

He was approached by a man one day saying angrily, "I gave you a twenty last week for the dog's meds. Didn't you get them for him?"

"Kidneys," replied Chris. He had well scripted lines. "He needs repeat meds."

"Oh!" said the man and put another ten-pound note into Chris' hat.

Fluffy was a picture of cuteness. A mixture of sad eyes and a tail wag. Fluffy seemed to know how to use his expressions and gestures to have maximum appeal. Even his name seemed to pull at heart strings.

"Don't know how you do it," commented Bill. Bill was one of the other homeless men who hung out under the bridge. "I've got a dog and they don't give me arf as much as you. You're a lucky bastard!" Bill had a Staffordshire bull terrier called Butch.

Stupid bastard, thought Chris. 'Fancy calling it Butch. Not exactly curb appeal.'

The name Fluffy sounded cute. When punters asked his name they greeted him with silly baby voices, "Ahhhh… Fluffy, that's so cute."

Chris grew closer to Fluffy than he ever wanted to admit. Fluffy had saved him. He still drank heavily but now he had new respect from the homeless community and could easily afford food and drink. At night he snuggled up to Fluffy in a real sleeping bag, not just a pile of rags. He was warm and happy. He even had the attention of woman. A homeless girl called Ruth had been hanging around him. He gave her cash sometimes. She was probably too young for him but Fluffy liked her and the company was nice.

Chris thought about trying to get a bedsit. Then he thought about his wife, his children, and Richard the prick from next door. Life was simpler on the street. He didn't have to try not to be useless. Noone was bothered. They were all useless. A bedsit would mean bills to pay, housework and responsibility. He was content not to have any of those things.

A small number of homeless people met under the bridge most of the days. It was dry under there and remote. Noone asked questions. Someone would disappear or a new face would join the gathering. No one ever asked where anyone had gone or where they'd come from. Chris knew he could be anyone. There would never be any pressure to be anything or do anything.

A new man, by the name of Mick had been hanging around on the outskirts of the group for a few weeks. No one had paid much attention. But one day, Mick drunk and aggressive came into the circle.

"Get that fucking dog out of here," he swayed and raised his fist. "I hate fucking dogs."

Chris felt his anger rising. "The dog stays. You get your fucking ass out of here."

The group moved, backing into the walls of the bridge, not wanting any part of the possible fight.

Without warning Mick kicked Fluffy viciously catching his leg. Fluffy yelped. Within seconds Chris lept forward and swung his fist into Mick's face. Mick seemed to sway but before Chris could take a second swing, Fluffy had leapt knocking Mick to the floor and tearing at Mick's leg.

"Fluffy no!" yelled Chris.

Fluffy continued to snarl and shook Mick's leg wildly. Chris grabbed Fluffy and somehow managed to detach him from the cowering Mick. Blood was oozing from Mick's leg but he managed to stand and hobble away. "Fucking thing should be put down!" yelled Mick as he left the group. "The fucking thing's mad!"

Fluffy continued to growl and snarl until Mick was out of sight. Chris felt a mixture of pride and concern. Clearly Fluffy had tried to protect him. Or at least, that was seemingly what had happened. Fluffy couldn't understand that Chris had already got the better of Mick.

But Chris was unnerved by the change in Fluffy. Not just his behaviour, his face as he bared his teeth and snarled. He turned from a cute cuddly dog into something resembling a monster. He was unrecognisable. His cute ears that rotated when he was being stroked were flattened to his head. He was normally obedient but Chris struggled to get him to listen. He was so fixated on attacking Mick that for those few minutes Chris hadn't existed.

The others had seen it, too. "Bloody hell!" said Bill. "Glad I ain't crossed you, I'd never have believed Fluffy would do that if I hadn't seen it. Bloody hell!" Bill shook his head in disbelief before moving his old blanket to the far end of the bridge. He wasn't going to sleep anywhere near Fluffy.

Before that incident most of the group would stroke Fluffy when Chris arrived. But afterwards many of the group kept their distance. No one bent to cuddle him. No one wanted to be anywhere near those teeth. In those few minutes Fluffy had caused an atmosphere of apprehension and fear amongst the homeless. Chris suspected that even those who hadn't witnessed the attack had been told that Fluffy could be vicious. When Chris nestled into his sleeping bag at night, he could be sure there would be no one close to him.

But the punters continued to be enchanted by Fluffy and Chris's enterprise continued to bear fruit. The incident faded into the back of Chris's drunken brain. Sometimes Chris tried to recall what had happened but it was muddled and he told himself it was nothing.

"We're a team Fluffy!" Chris told him. He wagged his tail and looked into Chris's face.

Fluffy never judged. When Chris fell over drunk, Fluffy would just lie by his side and lick his hand. When Chris thought about his past—his wife and children—he believed Fluffy loved him more than any one he ever had.

Ruth, the homeless girl continued to hang around Chris. Chris liked her. In fact, he was starting to like her a lot. She was young—too young.

"Where are your parents?" Chris asked her one day.

This was a total break in the unspoken rules of the homeless community. Each person was anonymous, invisible, it was what made them feel safe.

She looked at Chris with an expression of complete horror and he knew he should never have asked. Then he saw tears in her eyes.

"My father," she began but her voice faltered and she turned away. In that instant Chris knew why she was there. Her face told the story. She didn't need to say more.

He passed his bottle. She grabbed it and took a large gulp. They sat in silence with Fluffy nestled up to Chris on one side and Ruth on the other and fell into a drunken sleep.

Most nights, Ruth would lie next to Fluffy. Unlike the others, she wasn't frightened of Fluffy and Fluffy seemed to like her.

Sometimes, Chris would take Fluffy to an area the locals named it *The Plains*. It was a piece of waste ground that had been earmarked for development some years ago, but funds hadn't materialised, so it had been abandoned. It sat in an area between some high-rise flats and an industrial area. Sometimes, people would take a shortcut across the muddy, uneven land, but most of the time they'd use the road around the outside. Although the road was a longer route and[[it was perceived as a safer one. There were always people and traffic and you could arrive at your destination without being covered in mud or dust, so people didn't use The Plains frequently.

The Plains were also used by stray dogs or dogs that were locked out during the day by their working owners. There would be an occasional dog fight but nothing of significance. Most of the dogs played well together. There were probably several litters of puppies created on The Plains. People had fly-tipped rubbish over the years, a fridge, an old cooker, a few old cars were abandoned. Grass and weeds grew over them partially obscuring them and adding to the hazards for anyone taking a short cut

Fluffy would always get excited for a trip to The Plains. Chris would let him off the lead and he would run around with the other dogs, yelping and jumping over them. Chris would stand on the edge of The Plains watching and smiling at Fluffy's antics. Fluffy always came back when called. Sometimes a bit slow and reluctant to leave the game but he always came.

It was a spring morning and Chris had drunk more than usual. He decided to go to The Plains to clear his head. Ruth had followed Chris and they watched as Fluffy played with the other dogs. Chris was breathing the fresh air and smiling. Life was good.

Ruth moved closer to Chris. She reached into her pocket, pulled out a tiny package. "Open it," she said handing it over to Chris. He peeled back the fancy paper to reveal a woollen scarf. "I bought it for you," she said.

Then her words gushed out and he could see she was embarrassed. "I hope you like it. It doesn't matter if you donn't but I bought it. I didn't nick it or anything. I bought it proper like... I wanted you to have something from me.

Something to say thanks for looking out for me. Something… just something… but it's no big deal…"

"It's great," Chris interrupted her. "Just great!"

She looked at him with her sparkly eyes and smiled, "You really liked it?"

"It's the nicest present I have ever received," Chris said softly

Then she leant forward and kissed his cheek. He felt the softness of her lips on his skin and felt a sinking feeling in his stomach. What could he offer this beautiful young girl? He was useless and she was so fragile and vulnerable but he wanted to be near her, with her and protect her. He wanted to know her. She was different. She had spent her tiny bit of cash buying something for him. He felt embarrassed, grateful but as he looked at her, he felt a warmth inside which he hadn't thought he was capable of.

He reached into his pocket and his fingers found two twenty pound notes. "Tell you what," he said cheerfully. "Go get us a bottle. Good stuff. Not crap. I'll see you at the bridge in a couple of hours and we'll share a tot or two. Get some crisps too."

She gave him a quick, sidelong glance with a coy smile which made his heart flutter. He watched her walk away. He felt both elation and despair. This beautiful young woman was interested in him, but all he had to offer was a bottle and some crisps. In a different life he would take her to a fancy restaurant. He'd treat her to a new dress and they'd go back to his home and his bed, living a normal life.

Could he ever deserve this woman? Could he ever be anything like the person Ruth deserved? Chris had never tried to kiss Ruth or even hold her close. He knew her past and knew it would be difficult for her to be with someone.

The kiss that she planted on his cheek was a sign that she trusted Chris.

Chris didn't see the young woman enter The Plains. He was distracted by the thoughts of Ruth. The young woman was clearly in a hurry, half running with a pushchair in front of her. She was probably taking the short cut because she was late for something. She was stumbling over the rough ground and seemed to twist her ankle. She stopped for a moment and swore then bent to rub her ankle, straightened up and hurried off again.

The dogs were playing some distance away. It was Fluffy that seemed to spot her first. He stopped and stared with his paw in the air, almost as if he was pointing.

The next few minutes seemed like a slow motion film and Chris' smile faded into horror as he watched the event unfold in front of him. Fluffy ran swiftly towards the woman. Chris saw his face, snarling and ears flat. The poor woman didn't stand a chance. Already unsteady on the uneven ground, she was instantly knocked to the floor by Fluffy. Fluffy clenched her face in his mouth, crushing her skull with his strong jaw. The other dogs sensing a new game and began to grab the woman's whirling limbs as she fought to get free.

Chris heard the growling, yelping and an ear piercing scream. The screaming stopped and the woman seemed to lose consciousness as she stopped fighting back. Her arms flopped around as Fluffy shook her lifeless body, her face was still in his jaws. Her shoe flew off and up into the air. Another dog grabbed the shoe. Fluffy continued to rip at her face. The other dogs joined the assault grabbing her arms, legs, tearing every piece of cloth covering her body and making excited yelps.

Chris started running towards Fluffy, shouting, "Fluffy, here. Come here. Stop. Fluffy. For fucks sake, stop."

But Fluffy couldn't hear. His expressions were pure evil and he was locked into his own terrible game. Fluffy sensed the lack of movement and let go of the woman's head. He turned and saw an upturned pushchair and heard the cries of the infant. He launched into it and dragged something out. Chris could only see blankets but the other dogs were there too, pulling and tugging in their game of tug of war.

Chris reached the scene and dragged Fluffy away. The other dogs continued to sniff, chew and play with their spoils. There was blood and meat everywhere. The dogs were chewing on meat and eating up the woman's flesh.

Fluffy turned to Chris with his tail wagging. It was then Chris saw the baby's leg in Fluffy's mouth. "OH MY GOD! Fluffy, drop it!' Fluffy looked at him but didn't respond to Chris.

Chris hurriedly grabbed Fluffy by his collar, forcing his jaw open and threw the leg to the floor. He put Fluffy on his lead and ran like the wind away from the horrific scene. The other dogs remained chewing and snuffling in the bloody mess.

Chris ran to the old canal and washed the blood off Fluffy. He sat with his head in his hand. He was so tense that he completely forgot about Ruth. He was sweating as if he has been jogging for hours. He found a half bottle of rum in his pocket. He gulped it in seconds and then immediately felt sick—very sick.

Ruth sat by the bridge for hours, watching and waiting for Chris. He had given her money for whisky and crisps but she now knew he had paid her to go away and leave him alone. Rather than just telling her to fuck off, he'd paid her to go. Somehow that seemed worst. She felt stupid. She'd vowed never to let herself feel anything. *Stay numb. Don't think,* she thought.

She would have to leave this place now. Now that she felt humiliated and stupid. She could never look at Chris again. The other homeless people under the bridge knew she'd been hanging out with Chris so they'd all knew how stupid she'd been. She couldn't face the humiliation. Perhaps Chris was laughing at her. Perhaps he thought she was just a stupid young girl.

She put her hand into her coat pocket to pull out some crisps. A piece of paper stuck to her fingers. As she turned it over she realised it was the receipt for the scarf she had bought for Chris. She ripped it up and threw it on the floor.

She'd heard someone say there were rich pickings in Birmingham. She opened the bottle and took a large gulp. Then she got to her feet and began to walk.

Chris was drunk. Very drunk. He didn't know how long he'd been like this. He couldn't think or see straight. Images seemed to wave and dance in front of his eyes. Fluffy nestled by his side but Chris barely acknowledged him. He was in the station but he didn't have his hat in front of him. Occasionally someone approached to pat Fluffy but Chris growled from beneath his vomit stained coat.

"Leave my fucking dog alone!"

A newspaper fluttered in the wind and caught Chris' eye. He picked it up and through foggy eyes he started to read, *"A two month old baby had been ripped apart by a pack of dogs on The Plains. The mother was alive but faced years of surgery to restore what was left of her face. She also had extensive muscle damage and may lose her arm. The dogs had been rounded up and destroyed. The owners had been traced and all faced prosecution."*

But Chris knew they hadn't all been traced. Fluffy was very much alive and here with Chris. No one knew Chris' secret. No one knew Chris was harbouring a killer. No one seemed to have seen Chris flee the scene and if any of the homeless had suspicions about Chris' change of mood and behaviour they were unlikely to say. The homeless population didn't bond well with any authority. No one spoke to the police. But Chris still wondered. Was there a chance that someone may have seen something? Mick was still on the fringes of the group. Would he say something about an aggressive dog? Fluffy was distinctive. His white coat was unmistakeable, if anyone had witnessed the incident on The Plains they would have seen and remembered the white dog.

Chris couldn't decide whether he loved or hated Fluffy. He couldn't abandon him. There was a part of Chris that loved and cared for his only friend. But he didn't want to be around him either. Chris couldn't shake the thought of that baby's leg in Fluffy's mouth. He saw it continually through his drunken eyes, the blood trickling from the tiny limb, down Fluffy's white coat.

"You bastard!" he shouted through his tears. "You fucking bastard." But Fluffy didn't move an inch away. He continued to nestle up to Chris. And it was London. The land of the invisible. So all the passers-by kept passing by. Everyone was oblivious to Chris's tormented ranting.

In Chris's muddled thoughts, he decided to dump Fluffy away from him. Fluffy could be homeless somewhere else. He could be someone else's problem. Chris couldn't deal with this.

As Chris sobered slightly, he visited the chemist and bought two packets of black hair dye. He took Fluffy to the canal and poured the dye over his back and legs. After an hour, Fluffy was transformed into a slightly comical-looking black and white dog. If anyone had seen anything they would be looking for a white dog.

Chris bought a ticket to Yarmouth. He'd never been there, but it sounded okay and someone had told him there was a big dog rehoming centre there. It took him two days and a lot of walking to find the place. It wasn't the big rehoming centre Chris had been told about. In fact, it looked quite modest from the road. It was quite a way outside Yarmouth and Chris had walked for two hours to find the place. It was just getting dark. He tied a label to Fluffy's collar, saying simply 'Fluffy.'

Chris tied Fluffy's lead to the gate. But as he went to walk away, he felt a sudden rage. Fluffy had betrayed him. Just like his wife had betrayed him, he turned and kicked Fluffy.

Fluffy put his ears back, bared his teeth and snarled. He jerked forward, but the lead stopped him from biting Chris.

"Goodbye fucking Fluffy!" scowled Chris. He reached for the bottle of rum in his pocket and headed back towards the town. *Life is less complicated on your own,* he thought. *Just me and my bottle.*

He sang as he walked away, "Ho ho ho and a bottle of rum."

CHAPTER 4
ERIC'S STORY

Josy, the kennel maid, arrived to open the main gate to the rehoming centre. The owners Mr and Mrs Thomas, lived on site but left most of the work to Josy and Marie, the two kennel maids.

Josy didn't mind. She loved dogs and loved her job. Although she often felt sad and frustrated at the way people treated animals. She believed what she was doing was worthwhile. *No such thing as a bad dog, only a bad owner,* she thought.

Josy had only once been bitten. A small frightened dog attacked and bit Josy's hand, but only once. Within a week, Josy had turned the animal into a placid puppy. Although she had refused to rehome the dog to a family with small children, she was convinced that the middle-aged couple who took the dog would be able to provide a suitable home.

Occasionally, people brought dogs back. Josy always told anyone who came to rehome a dog that they could return the dog if it didn't work out. She believed it was better that they did this rather than struggle, making themselves and the dog unhappy. She thought that there was a right home for every dog. Her job was to find it.

The kennels were well advertised, so they were successful at rehoming. The longest period a dog had ever been there was nine months.

Occasionally, a dog had to be put down. But this was always because of health issues. Josy had never had a dog which was so aggressive that careful training failed. Some were a bit temperamental, so she would recommend using a muzzle in public and only rehome those dogs to experienced owners and adult families.

Despite the notices on the gate advising that dogs would be accepted without question, it wasn't unusual for dogs to be left abandoned and tied to the gate.

So here was another dog.

"Hello," she said softly. She offered her hand. Not too close. She didn't want to be bitten. But it was obvious that this dog posed no threat. It wagged its tail as she approached and let out an excited yelp.

He had the most beautiful face and eyes that seemed to look straight into Josy's soul. The kennels were full, but Josy would always find a space. She would have to juggle as she couldn't put a new dog in with another and needed to make sure the new dog was friendly with other dogs. She had already paired the obvious ones, so finding space for the newcomer would be a challenge.

Josy was overweight. Her shoulder-length brown hair was scraped back into a ponytail, which hung down, looking like a rat's tail. She wore thick glasses and no makeup. She smelt of a wet dog but didn't care. She was content. She loved her job. It was her dream job. The pay was poor, but Josy never wanted to do anything else.

The dog was beautiful. Black and white with appealing eyes. Josy fell in love with his smile.

As she was untying the lead from the gate, an elderly man came around the corner. Before Josy could stop him, the dog lunged and pulled free.

Josy, alarmed, tried to grab the dog, but she need not have worried. The dog bounded over to the man but stopped short, so as not to knock him over. Still wagging it's tail, it nestled up to him. Then he circled the man, just like a show dog, sat in front of him and offered his paw.

"I'm so sorry," said Josy as she tried to pick up the lead.

The dog, excited, was wagging his tail so hard that his whole body wagged. But he was also gentle and didn't push or knock the elderly man.

The man accepted the dog's paw. "Pleased to meet you," he said smiling.

"He's been abandoned," Josy explained. "Left tied to the gate." She picked up his lead and examined his collar.

"Fluffy!" she read. "So your name is Fluffy."

"Well, Fluffy. Let's get you inside and give you some food and water."

"He's beautiful!" exclaimed the man, looking at Fluffy with eyes full of love. "What will happen to him?"

"We'll get him some food and water, check him over, then put him up for rehoming."

"Trouble is," Josy said out loud but to herself. "Kennels are full. I'm not quite sure where I can put him at the moment. It shouldn't take too long to home him, though.

He's cute and obviously affectionate. Doesn't look like a problem pooch."

"I'm Eric," said the man, offering his hand. "I pass here some days. I live on the hill. I like to walk around the woods, but I come down here sometimes just for a change. I've seen you lots of times."

Josy didn't think anyone lived on the hill and she didn't recall seeing the man before. But Josy wasn't good in the mornings. She usually felt half asleep when she came to work and stayed that way until she'd had a strong coffee. The man was insignificant. Just an old man, flat cap, baggy trousers, brown shoes and a faded sports jacket. He was a little on the thin side but looked fairly fit. He carried a walking stick but didn't look as if he needed to use it.

No wonder Josy hadn't noticed him. There wasn't much to notice.

"I'm Josy," she shook Eric's hand and turned to walk away. But Fluffy held back, clearly reluctant to come.

"So do you own the kennels?" Eric asked.

The last thing Josy wanted was a long conversation. But Fluffy was pulling back and Eric seemed intent on engaging Josy with idle chat.

During the next thirty minutes, Josy tried numerous times to turn away without being rude. But Eric seemed to latch on, probably lonely, Josy thought and Fluffy had glued himself to Eric. Josy knew the only way she was going to move Fluffy was by dragging him across the ground which is not easy with such a big dog.

She tried the usual high-pitched voice. "Come on, Fluffy. Let's get you some nice din dins. What a lovely doggy doo!" But Fluffy was having none of it. He just moved behind Eric, making capture more difficult.

Josy was just about to ask Eric if he would consider helping to settle Fluffy into a kennel when Eric said, "You say you've got no room. Well, I've got room. I could take him."

Josy thought for a moment. Highly irregular. But she really didn't know where to put Fluffy. Then there was the paperwork. Fluffy would need to be signed in, checked and adverts for any possible owners would need to be placed before he could be rehomed. All this was tedious, lengthy, but standard procedure, even though it was obvious that Fluffy had been abandoned.

Anyway, Josy thought. *Some dogs seem to pick their own owners.*

Josy was getting desperate for her coffee. She was now very late. The dogs in the kennels were beginning to howl.

"Are you sure about this?" Josy asked. "You must bring him back if there are any problems."

Eric looked at Fluffy. "I'm sure," he said with a determined voice.

So, with a shake of the hand and a wave, Josy disappeared into the gate in a hurry to get on with her day. Eric watched her go and waved, wondering what had just happened and what he had just done.

For some unknown reason, Eric had decided to walk to the village that morning rather than walk around the woods. He had thought he might buy a pint of milk at the shop. He never needed much. He had his usual small bag of groceries delivered once a fortnight and paid cash. He had a bank account where his pension was paid and his savings were kept. Every three months he would go to the bank in the village and draw out enough cash to pay for his groceries. He kept the cash in a box under a loose floorboard.

Fifteen years ago he had been working in a bank in the town. At sixty, he was called into the office and offered early retirement. The bank manager clearly didn't see a position for Eric in his new style bank.

Eric struggled to embrace the new technology; he still used a calculator and was always being chastised for taking too long and talking to customers. He was the oldest employee and didn't seem to look comfortable in the new uniforms, which consisted of brightly coloured tee shirts. He kept forgetting to put his badge on, which read, "My name is Eric and I'm here to help." The badge was too big and dug into his nipple when he bent over.

And he hated the informality. When he first started working at the bank, there was respect. Customers called him Mr Knight and he addressed them by their correct titles. Now, everyone was encouraged to speak to him as if he was their best mate.

Eric lived in a flat, walking distance from the bank and had moved there after his mother had died. He had never married and only had a couple of fleeting attempts at romance. The flat had been new when he moved there. A place to call home and make a private space for himself. But now most of the flats were owned by a housing company. They rented the flats to young people who seemed unable to sleep. The flat seemed to vibrate with the sound of something the youngsters called music.

Eric had been walking down the road in a daze, wondering what to do, when he glanced in an Estate Agent's window and there it was. An odd-looking place with no main electricity and a well. Eric arranged to view it and fell in love with it.

Eric was fed up with modern life. The house on the hill was surrounded by woodland and isolated. The nearest neighbours were over a mile away. There was a small village a mile away. It had a shop, a post office, which doubled as a bank. A small pub and not much else.

When Eric viewed the house, he sat in the doorway and knew he had found his home. So he left his job, his flat and his old life behind and started a new, peaceful life, living on his own terms.

It hadn't all been plain sailing. He had to have a pump installed so that he could shower and more recently, he had been forced to arrange grocery and fuel deliveries. As he aged, the trips to the shop became more difficult. But he was fit and happy. He never craved human company and quickly learnt about the birds and animals which shared his space on the hill. He put up nest boxes and planted a few vegetables.

So why had he now offered to take on a dog? What on earth had he been thinking to come up with this idea? *I'm going mad,* Eric said to himself.

Fluffy seemed to really like him and Eric believed he had a bond with all animals. Fluffy was pretty, too. Unusual black patches on his back and legs, and those eyes. Okay, lots of dogs have nice eyes, but there was something different, something special.

Fluffy walked with him back to his home. He didn't pull on the lead and seemed completely pleased to plod along at Eric's side. When Eric opened the door, Fluffy was instantly at home. He lay by the fireplace and looked as if he'd always lived there.

Eric suddenly had the feeling that there had been an empty place in his life and it had just been filled. It was like something was missing, but he wasn't aware of what it was. Eric had thought he was happy. Now, he believed he was truly happy. The dog looked like it was meant to be there.

Over the next few weeks, Fluffy became Eric's constant companion. Fluffy loved to bound through the trees and brought Eric sticks to throw. They went on long walks together. When Eric wanted to watch birds, Fluffy would sit quietly, his ears pricked as if he were watching them. Eric didn't think he had ever smiled so much.

Once, while out walking, Fluffy found a young bird. It wasn't injured and had fallen from it's nest. Fluffy nudged it with his nose but never attempted to bite it or harm it. Eric was able to pick the bird up and return it to it's nest.

"You are a truly gentle soul," Eric told Fluffy.

Fluffy had been with Eric for a few months when Eric noticed the change. Fluffy had been a black and white dog but Eric noticed Fluffy was more white than black. Eric dismissed it with a smile.

"My hair turned white too," he told Fluffy. "You are still a very handsome dog."

Eric had no idea of Fluffy's age. But Fluffy seemed healthy and happy, so it didn't matter.

As Christmas approached, Eric developed a strange sense of excitement, which he hadn't felt since he was a child.

Normally, Christmas was the only time of the year when he felt sad.

Eric felt as if Christmas Day should be special, but no matter how he tried, it was much the same as any other day. He always tried to make himself a Christmas dinner and bought a nice bottle of wine. He even wore a paper hat, but each year, a sense of disappointment and sadness crept over him and he was glad when Christmas had passed and he could return to his normal existence.

But this year was different. He had Fluffy.

Eric cut a small tree from the wood and dragged it inside. He made tree decorations out of foil wrappings saved from his grocery delivery. He ordered wine, turkey and meat, which he could share with Fluffy. And best of all, he ordered some presents for Fluffy. Two squeaky toys and three of his favorite chews. He had also managed to order, with the help of the lady in the shop, a special present—an engraved dog tag. It said 'Fluffy.' He wrapped them up.

On Christmas Eve, he put them under the tree before he and Fluffy went to bed.

On Christmas morning, Fluffy went straight to the presents and, one at a time, dragged them into the middle of the room. It was as if he knew it was Christmas. He then proceeded to rip the paper excitedly, wagging his tail and making little yelping noises.

Eric had never laughed so much in years. Fluffy was clearly delighted and Eric was glad that he had made the effort to celebrate Christmas properly. Eric put Fluffy's new dog tag onto his collar and Fluffy paraded around the room as if showing off his new necklace.

Fluffy played with his squeaky toys all morning, running from one toy to the other. Squeaking one after another and when Eric went to a different room, Fluffy followed him, bringing both toys in turn.

Eric cooked a turkey crown and a small piece of beef. Eric tucked into a Christmas dinner while Fluffy tucked into a bowl of freshly cooked meat. Eric wore a homemade paper hat. When Eric sat on the chair after dinner, Fluffy ran around the back of the chair and playfully snatched Eric's hat, running around with it in his mouth until it was too soggy to use.

In the early evening, they went for their usual walk and saw a large tawny owl just as the light faded.

When Eric and Fluffy went to bed that night, Eric thought he had just had the best day of his life with his best friend.

CHAPTER 5
MICHELLE'S STORY

Pain. Michelle woke in pain. She couldn't open her eyes. Or were they open? Was she dreaming? A voice came from nearby, "I think she's waking up." Then nothing.

Dreams. Little George. A dog. A white dog. A ripping sensation and pain. Darkness. Black. Red. But always the dog. The big white snarling dog. Then nothing.

She could see. Not well, but just a slit. What could she see? A woman. Possibly a nurse. The woman came closer.

"Hello. You're awake?"

Michelle tried to respond but her voice came out as a croak.

"It's okay, just relax. You've been through a lot. You need to rest."

But Michelle's mind was racing. White dog. Ripping. Pain and George. Where was her baby George? The croak came again, but she wouldn't give up. She tried to mouth the words. Tried to raise her head.

"Orge. Orge," she whispered in pain. She took a huge breath and with every ounce of strength she could gather, she screamed, "Where's George?"

The nurse looked at her with a concerned expression. "I'll get the doctor."

Then she disappeared from her sight. Had she understood? Where had she gone? When would she be back? Was she alone? But most of all, where was George? Tears started flowing down the side of her eyes. She was worried for her baby. Her heart pounded in her chest and she began to feel sick as she pieced together the events.

She had seen the pack of dogs approaching. At first, she had thought that they were just a noisy nuisance, but as they approached she had seen the white dog leading the pack. It looked like a rabid beast, snarling, drooling and making a gut-churning noise between a growl and a roar. It jumped and bit straight into her face. She felt the flesh tearing and as he increased the pressure, her eye popped.

Her vision was blurred and she couldn't see things properly no matter how she tried. She tried to lift her arm to feel her face, but her arms were too heavy and painful. She couldn't remember seeing George. Where was George? If the dogs had attacked her, then George must be okay. So, who was caring for him? Michelle was a single parent. She had split up with her boyfriend before George was born, but her mum and younger sister lived nearby. They'd be caring for George. George would be okay with her mum.

It seemed an eternity until the doctor appeared. He shone a light into her eyes and listened to her chest. He told her she had a lot of stitches in her arms and legs, so it was best not to try to move too much. He asked if she had remembered what had happened. Her voice was a rasp that she didn't recognise. Her throat was painful, but she told him she remembered being attacked by a pack of dogs led by a white dog. It was difficult to talk, but she kept asking, "Where's George?"

He stood, smoothed his coat and said, "We've called your mum. She's on her way. Try to rest for now." Then he left the room.

She closed her eyes, thinking that her mum would bring George.

When she woke, her mother was sitting by her bed crying. Her sister, Tina, also had tears in her eyes and appeared to be trying to hold back. To begin with, Michelle thought it was her appearance. She must look dreadful. She knew the dog had ripped at her face. But when she asked, "Where's George?" her mother's face crumpled and she shook her head.

Then Michelle knew. It hit her like a bolt. The scream came through her gravelly throat and seemed to fill the whole room and her head. Her mother put her head on the bed next to her, weeping. The doctor came rushing into the room and injected her with something. She barely felt the needle in her vein and within minutes she blacked out.

Michelle's injuries were horrendous. She had lost a lot of blood and for a while, it was doubtful that she would pull through. Her injuries included a broken ankle, a broken arm, numerous lacerations and bites all over her body, particularly to her left arm where part of the muscle had been torn away and probably eaten by one of the dogs, but the worst were her facial injuries. She had lost one eye. Clear, deep teeth marks showed around her forehead. There wasn't much left of her nose and her cheek had been torn away, exposing her jaw and her teeth. Part of her ear was missing too. She was unrecognisable and looked hideous.

Even as the injuries began to heal, it was obvious that the injuries would be permanently life-changing. Her disfigured arm could not support any weight. So, even holding a cup of tea was impossible with the left hand. Her speech was slurred. Even after extensive physiotherapy, she was always going to walk with a limp. She was never going to recover sufficiently to have a normal life.

The worst was her face. Her nose made a snorting noise as she tried to breathe. Her good eye, if you could call it that, looked droopy, and her missing cheek meant that the left side of her jaw was continually exposed—she looked like a monster.

Various doctors and consultants came to offer their opinions, but this wasn't a question of closing wounds. The dogs had eaten parts of her face and there wasn't enough flesh left to repair. They discussed skin grafts, but the general consensus was that even with years of extensive skin grafts, Michelle was unlikely to ever resemble a normal woman.

One day, a detective came to see Michelle. He looked at her with tears in his eyes. He told her he had wanted to see her. He was one of the first on the scene following the attack. Michelle wanted to know everything. Somehow, the information seemed important to her. Detective Numan told her that George's death would have been quick. He was a tiny baby and probably died from the first bite, but Michelle wanted to know more and kept asking.

Eventually, he thought it best to tell her the truth. George's tiny body had been mostly devoured by the dogs and for that reason, she would be unable to view his body.

They had released the body for a funeral, but a date hadn't been set. They were waiting to see if Michelle would be well enough to attend.

Detective Numan explained that all the dogs had been rounded up and destroyed. There were seven in total and most lived on the same estate as Michelle. Michelle thought with dismay that she must have walked past these dog owners and may need to do so again when she was discharged from the hospital. But it was the white dog that haunted Michelle's dreams. He was clearly the leader of the pack and the one who had been responsible for most of Michelle's injuries. "And the white dog. Who owned the white dog?" she asked curiously.

Detective Numan looked at Michelle, confused. "Michelle," he said softly. "There was no white dog."

Michelle looked back in horror. "But there was one. I'm certain. He was the leader. He was a big, fluffy, white dog."

Detective Numan still wasn't sure. Michelle's injuries were so severe it was highly likely that she had poor recall of the attack. They had arrived on the scene soon after the attack. They had been called by a resident in the flats, which overlooked the ground. When the police arrived, the dogs were still there, excited. They were still chewing on bones and meat. Most of the police officers attending the scene had vomited and several had requested counselling. It seemed unlikely that any of the dogs had just wandered off.

The resident had seen the attack and immediately went to her phone to call the police. The phone wasn't near the window, so she hadn't stopped to watch. She couldn't say how many dogs were there or give a description.

House-to-house inquiries hadn't produced any other witnesses and although all expressed horror at what had happened, many seemed reluctant to get involved. Most residents knew at least one of the dog owners. Some residents often left their own dogs to fend for themselves and run unsupervised over The Plains, so didn't want to sit in judgement of the dog owners. And no one knew of a large white dog living on the estate. There was a white dog owned by Mrs Jack in the bottom flat, but it turned out to be a very old small Jack Russell cross, which seemed to struggle to venture outside for a pee.

Michelle was discharged from the hospital after sixteen weeks. There seemed no point in keeping her there. She still returned for her wounds to be checked and for follow-up appointments where consultants tried and failed to find a suitable treatment plan. She took strong painkillers but still seemed aware and alert. She never stopped talking about the large white dog, which she claimed had led the pack and been largely responsible for her injuries and the death of her little boy. The white dog would haunt her every night when she went to sleep. Her brain couldn't rest until she found the dog.

Shortly after Michelle's discharge, the funeral was held. Detective Numan was there with tears in his eyes as the tiny coffin sat at the front of the church. Numan couldn't help wondering what was in the coffin. Bones, even some of those, had been crunched and swallowed. Bits of unidentifiable meat and half a head, the brains had been dragged out and chewed. Numan felt sick just thinking about it. Michelle desperately wanted to see what was left of her little boy, but mercifully, her mother intervened and Michelle relented. No one should ever have to see what was left of Michelle's sweet baby boy.

Numan looked around the church. It was packed. Many people from the town had turned out, not just from the estate but from the wider community. Michelle stood at the front of the church wearing a long black coat and a thick black veil. She was devastated. If they had of been able to see her face they could not have seen her feelings. Her half-torn face could not smile, frown so the devestation would never be seen. Those who stood close to her could hear the noise coming from under the veil. Her nose and throat made normal crying impossible. The sobs came in a series of snorts and rasps, which sounded more like an animal.

No one noticed the homeless drunken man hanging around at the door of the church. And no one noticed that he was crying as the congregation filed out.

A few days later, another homeless man, Mick, watched as Chris laid a droopy bunch of flowers on baby George's grave. And at that moment, another person knew the truth—Mick. He knew what exactly happened to baby George. Mick was sure something was fishy as Chris's white dog was missing, and now he was laying flowers on the baby's grave.

Chris hadn't found easy pickings in Yarmouth. Police frequently moved him on when he tried to beg on the seafront. So he decided to return to London, where he could be invisible. He still had nightmares and saw the baby's leg in Fluffy's mouth. When he heard about the funeral, he was drawn to the churchyard and watched from a distance with tears in his eyes.

He visited the tiny grave when no one was around and took flowers. Most of them were acquired from other graves. Chris reasoned that George deserved them more than anyone else. Sometimes, he would pick some from a garden when most people were in bed. Then, he'd say a prayer for George as he laid the flowers and begged for forgiveness.

A week after baby George's funeral, Mick wandered into the police station and asked to see the policeman in charge of the dog attack. He smelled of drink body odour and filth. The desk sergeant had told the man the case was closed.

"No, it ain't," the man said. "I got something interesting to tell," Mick swayed and tilted his head upwards, looking arrogant.

"You can tell me, Mr..."

"Me name's Mick. And I ain't talkin to you. I want your bossman."

"He isn't in," stated the sergeant.

"I'll wait," Mick said, taking a seat in the waiting area.

Mick stank really bad. And it was obvious that he had nowhere to go. He was likely to sit until the station closed and return when it opened. Perhaps Numan would just see him for a couple of seconds to get rid of him. The desk sergeant went upstairs to find Numan.

"Boss, sorry, but there's a homeless chap in the front wanting to see the guy in charge of the dog attack. He won't go and won't speak to me. He stinks really bad. I know I shouldn't ask, but could you give him a few seconds so that he goes peacefully on his way. I'm going to run out of air fresheners if he stays much longer."

Numan sighed. He wasn't exactly busy, but this chap probably wanted to report seeing a Yorkshire Terrier in the area. Something completely useless, but he might as well see him. It would save a scuffle in reception when they tried to evict the chap. He'd play along and hopefully, the man would leave quietly and go back to wherever he'd come from.

Numan headed to the reception. Mick was sitting with his feet crossed and looking very comfortable. He really did smell bad and the stench had filled the room.

"You wanted to talk to me," said Numan.

"Nah," drawled Mick. "You want to talk to me."

"The case is closed," said Numan, turning to walk away. "All the owners have been traced and are facing prosecution. Two have already been to court and all the dogs have been destroyed."

Numan was nearly through the door when Mick said, "Not all the dogs."

Numan turned. "What do you mean?"

"Ah!" said Mick. "I've got your attention."

"So you're thinking one might have got away," Numan said raising his left brow.

Mick grinned and picked at his teeth with a long, dirty fingernail.

"You're talking rubbish," said Numan. "You'll have to give me more than that."

"I've got reason to believe, Mr Policeman," Mick smiled sarcastically. "That one got away!"

"Okay," said Numan, turning back into the room. "I'll need a description of the dog, location and why you think he was involved."

"It's a nasty bastard," said Mick, rolling up his trouser leg. "He nearly had me, but I'm a big, strong chap, so I could fight him off."

Numan couldn't see much of Mick's leg. He couldn't tell if there were any marks. Mick was filthy and Numan wasn't going to get any closer.

"Description?" said Numan abruptly.

"But what's in it for me?" asked Mick with a sinister smile creeping across his face.

Numan started to lose patience.

"A baby was killed!" Numan was outraged. "And you're saying you want money for information. You make me sick!" Numan headed for the door.

"White," Mick said. "A big white dog. But I ain't sayin' no more unless you give me a tenner."

Numan froze. "You'd better come through."

It cost Numan twenty pounds out of his own pocket to get Mick to give the information. But a few hours later, Numan was prowling the streets, looking in doorways for a man in a blue overcoat called Chris.

Numan didn't find Chris that day, nor the next.

On the third day, he received a phone call from Michelle's mum.

"Please can you come and have a chat with her, Detective Numan. She won't stop talking about this white dog. She's obsessed with it. I don't know whether what she's saying is right, but it's driving me mad. She thinks no one is bothered and she says it killed George. I told her a million times that all the dogs were gone, but she won't have it. She's screaming and shouting like it's my fault. She's talking about going to the press. I can't take much more."

"It's okay," said Numan. "I might have a bit of news. I'll come over and talk to her."

Numan entered the grubby flat now shared by Michelle, her sister Tina, and her mum. Michelle hadn't been back to her own flat since the attack and it seemed unlikely that Michelle would be able to live on her own.

As Michelle came into the room, Numan tried not to wince and back away. The left side of her face was gone, showing just exposed teeth and bone. What was left of the skin was thin and yellow and seemed to hang in patches. She didn't look human. As she struggled to breathe and talk, rasping noises came from the hole that was once her nose and saliva dribbled down her front jaw.

Numan had been to the flat before when Michelle was in hospital. He had noted the photos on the fireplace of Michelle and Tina together smiling. They were both pretty girls. Tina was blond and Michelle brunette but the features were so striking and similar. Apart from the hair colouring, they could have been twins. The photos were missing now. They were removed. How could any of them bear to look at those photos ever again?

"The white dog!" rasped Michelle. "You've given up looking."

"It's not that," Numan started, but Michelle silenced him with a wave of her hand.

"It needs to be found," Michelle stated w. She turned her head away and said quietly with more clarity than Numan thought possible. "I need to find him. For George, for me. For this!" she gestured to her face. Numan saw a tear escape from her droopy eye.

At that moment, Numan knew he was going to break every rule in the book to give this wretched creature some comfort she needed.

"I'll tell you everything I know," said Numan.

He sat on the sofa and began to tell Michelle about a drunken homeless man who claimed to have information about a white dog.

The next day Michelle asked her mother to call her a taxi. She was going to the city. Michelle's mother objected and begged her not to go, but Michelle was determined and her mother wondered whether this might be progress. Michelle had refused to go out even to the bin, so this new determination might be the start of a return to some sort of normality.

Michelle took her walking stick. She was in obvious pain and struggled to hold the stick and walk, but she hobbled to the taxi wearing her long coat and thick veil.

She spoke to the taxi driver just once to give him the location, near the river where Numan had told her homeless people go to congregate. The taxi driver, seeing the veil and hearing the rasps, thought she was probably in mourning, so he didn't try to engage her in conversation. He was slightly curious when she paid. He saw her mangled hand. He offered her change, but she told him to keep it. Michelle was struggling to grip anything and didn't want to be bothered trying to pocket the change.

Michelle wandered around for three hours. She saw lots of homeless people but no one matching the description of Chris. Her pain was getting worse. She was thirsty but couldn't go to a cafe. She would have to sort change or might drop the cup or worse. She would have to lift her veil to drink and knew she looked like a monster. She was just about to give up her search and struggle towards the nearest taxi rank when she spotted him. She was surprised to see that he matched the description exactly—big blue coat, shaggy hair and always a bottle in his hand.

She approached him cautiously. "Chris," she said gently.

He lifted his head. "Who wants to know?" there was aggression in his voice.

"I'm Michelle," she said as if he would know. Would he know? Would he have bothered to find out anything about the people his dog had attacked, assuming it was his dog? Numan only had the account of another drunken homeless man.

"I've come to talk to you about your dog," she said gently.

"I ain't got no fucking dog. Now piss off!"

Michelle bent down in front of Chris so that he couldn't avoid her face. Then she lifted her veil. Chris gasped in horror. Stared for a moment, then put his head down and sobbed loud, racking sobs that shook his whole body.

"You have to give him up, Chris." She touched his arm. "Chris, he'll do it again. You need to give him up."

"I hate him," Chris sobbed. Snot and tears ran down his face. "That bastard, that fucking bastard. I hate him. I didn't believe he'd do something like that. I would never…" His voice trailed off. He couldn't speak. He'd run out of words. There were no words. He sobbed loudly like a child—an inconsolable child.

Chris tilted his head up. His eyes closed. He couldn't look at her, but he nodded between his sobs. Michelle took out her mobile phone. Numan picked up and heard the rasp.

"Michelle?" he said curiously.

"Numan, I've found Chris. He's ready to talk to us."

Chris agreed to come to the police station. He seemed exhausted. Numan promised him a warm cell and some hot food and drink.

Chris had been afraid he would be prosecuted for owning a dangerous dog, but now, he didn't care. He was broken and missed Fluffy more than he could admit. Fluffy had been all Chris had, and if Fluffy hated the world, so did Chris. And anyway, he was still convinced that if Fluffy hated everyone else, he loved Chris. They had a bond, and Chris felt as if he had betrayed that bond. But when Chris saw the poor woman in front of him, he couldn't hide anymore. Fluffy had turned her into something inhuman. He had taken her life. He had killed her baby. She had survived, but she could never live a normal life.

So slowly, through tears, Chris told them everything. But he also told them how Fluffy licked his hand, kept him warm and became a true friend. He told them he had taken the dog miles away and described the place as best he could remember. He told them he didn't believe his dog was vicious. He said he had been egged on by other dogs. When they asked what he called him, he said simply, "Friend, he was my friend."

Chris couldn't bring himself to say Fluffy's name. That would have been the last act of betrayal. He had abandoned Fluffy in a strange place and given him away. Now, he had given away the secret location. It could end Fluffy's life. So he couldn't go that last step and give away his name. "He was just my friend," Chris said to himself.

Numan arranged for Chris to be taken into custody and promised to provide him with a warm bed and some food for just one night. It would give him time to think. Chris nestled as best he could on the hard bed in the cell and tried to sleep. It may have been the lack of alcohol or the vivid nightmares, but Chris screamed all night. The custody sergeant couldn't wait to throw Chris out the next morning.

Numan took the day off work to take Michelle to Yarmouth. He knew his bosses wouldn't approve. Numan had tried to argue to keep the case open, but everyone wanted to believe that all the dogs had been caught and Michelle's recollection was bound to be inaccurate. Wasn't the expression, *Let sleeping dogs lie?*

Having consulted the map and the local business index, they found that there were two possible rehoming centres in the area. They pulled up at the first one just after midday. Josy looked up as they walked through the gate.

"Hi, are you looking for a dog?" she smiled.

"Yes, but a particular dog," Numan replied.

Josy looked at the strange couple and wondered if they belonged to a weird religion. The woman's head was completely covered, even her eyes weren't visible.

"Have you lost one?"

"Yes," Numan replied quickly before Michelle could respond. He thought it best not to say they were looking for a killer dog. Much better to play on heartstrings.

"We lost our dog nearly twelve months ago, but we've never given up and were told he could have been in this area."

"We've had a lot of dogs in twelve months," said Josy.

"This was a rather large white dog."

"Oh," Josy smiled. "I'm really sorry, but I don't think we've had a large white dog. That's not a common sort of description. Most dogs have a bit of white in them and there are a few pure white little ones, but large white dogs aren't that common. I can have a look down our records, but I think I would have remembered."

Numan asked her to check anyway. Josy ran her finger down the three pages of the book, which covered the last twelve months.

"Nothing, I'm afraid," she said.

"Well, if you do have one handed in, can you call me?"

Numan handed Josy his card. Josy eyed it with surprise. "You're a policeman," she stated.

"It's just my job and that's the easiest way to get hold of me," Numan smiled.

"Okay, I'll keep my eyes open," smiled Josy as they left.

Weird, thought Josy. *A policeman and a wife wrapped like a mummy. Looked like she was in hiding.*

The same story came from the second kennel, so with reluctance, Numan and Michelle headed home.

The trail had gone cold. The dog could be anywhere.

But in fact, the dog was just a mile away, strolling through the woods with a stick in his mouth, and Eric was wandering along, enjoying the peace and the company. Fluffy was wagging his tail, looking for all the world like a best friend would look.

Perhaps if the description had been a large black and white dog, it may have triggered a thought in Josy's mind, but there had certainly been no large white dogs. Fluffy was safe.

CHAPTER 6
ERIC

Eric and Fluffy had been together for just over twelve months. Fluffy was now a beautiful, pure white dog. Fluffy ran in the woods, paddled in the puddles, swam in the stream and rolled in anything that smelt bad. He always washed himself in the nearby stream when he came home, so he kept his white fur in a splendid condition. Eric did help by grooming Fluffy regularly, an experience they both seemed to enjoy.

Once, when Eric had a bad stomach, Fluffy took himself out for his usual morning pee, but he didn't go far. He was back within five minutes and seemed to make more of a fuss than ever of Eric. It seemed that he knew something was wrong, so he cuddled up to Eric even closer.

Fluffy never showed any sign of aggression. Eric enjoyed watching the wildlife and had once come across a muntjac, grazing in the clearing. He put his finger to his lips, "Hush Fluffy."

Fluffy dutifully lay at Eric's side, silently watching the animal until it moved away and they resumed their walk. Fluffy made no attempt to chase or frighten the animal.

Fluffy had once brought a rabbit back. It was a baby and flopped in Fluffty's mouth. But Eric hadn't seen Fluffy kill the rabbit, so he reasoned that it was probably dead already. He even thought Fluffy might have brought it back in the hope that Eric could save it. Fluffy watched all the wildlife with Eric. He seemed to enjoy simply watching. Eric had never even heard Fluffy growl.

Eric led a carefree life with Fluffy. He didn't want or need any other company.

When the fuel ran out, he phoned a local company which delivered his oil. When he needed groceries, he phoned for a delivery. Eric rarely went to the shop. Once or twice he ran out of essential so took the route that took him past the kennel where he had found Fluffy. Once, he thought he might try to speak to the girl he met, 'Josy' he seemed to recall. He thought he might have thanked her for giving her such a wonderful friend, but she was probably busy.

When the delivery drivers came, Eric always kept a distance from them, refusing to engage in conversation. He didn't like people and now that he had Fluffy, any human contact felt like an intrusion.

He even altered his diet, eating more tinned food so that he didn't have to put up with frequent grocery deliveries. Sometimes, he could go three weeks without a delivery and without seeing anyone. Fluffy was his life and all he needed.

Eric planted a few carrots and onions in the patch of ground outside his bungalow. As he was digging a hole, he looked across to find Fluffy digging furiously. He laughed so much at how Fluffy seemed to be trying to help.

When Eric repaired the porch on the bungalow, Fluffy helped, carrying wood and even passing Eric a screwdriver. If anyone had been watching, they would have thought Fluffy was highly trained, but Eric marvelled that he had never had to train Fluffy. Fluffy just seemed to know things.

It's love, Eric thought. *When you love something and it loves you back. You have a connection. Fluffy always seemed to know what to do.*

It was a cold day when Fluffy and Eric set off for their usual walk. They normally took one of four regular routes. The routes Eric took through the woods were not on a path or well-trodden. Eric knew the woods well, so he was able to explore the isolated parts. The route he decided on this morning took them towards the stream. The big river was near, but today was cold and Eric didn't think it would be good for Fluffy to attempt a swim and decided to walk by the stream. Fluffy liked to paddle his feet and Eric thought he had heard a nightingale there recently, so they set off as usual. Fluffy weaving in and out of the trees and bushes but never too far away. He disappeared just for a moment behind a dense, thick bush.

It was when he emerged that Eric couldn't believe his eyes.

Fluffy's face had changed. His ears were flat against his head and his teeth were bared in a snarl. It didn't look like Fluffy. It was Fluffy's face, but it was so different. Those beautiful, sad eyes had narrowed and were now staring. His ears were flat against his head and his lovely, soft mouth now displayed gnashing, snarling teeth. Drool dribbled from his mouth in a long streak of slime.

"Fluffy?" Eric said in disbelief. He glanced behind him. Fluffy couldn't actually be growling at him, but Eric couldn't see anything or anyone else.

As he turned his head back, Fluffy leapt, attacking with his sharp, firm teeth around Eric's throat. Eric's arms flailed and he attempted to shout, but he couldn't breathe.

Fluffy shook violently. It was all over in a couple of short minutes. Fluffy had ripped Eric's throat out. He now proceeded to bite and chew at his arms and legs, dragging Eric's lifeless body across the rough ground and under the bush.

Fluffy continued the vicious attack, consuming bits of flesh, which he tore away with his strong jaws. Then suddenly, he seemed to lose interest and trotted away, wagging his tail and looking like someone's lost family pet.

Soon, the rain began, slow at first but then heavier, washing clean the blood-stained ground. Eric's hat remained in the open but would soon be covered by leaves and debris.

It would be many years before Eric's rotting corpse would be discovered—unrecognisable, unidentified, unknown. Who would miss the old man on the hill? Most people didn't even know he existed and no one really cared. Eric didn't have a friend in the world.

Over the years, Eric's old, run-down bungalow was battered by the wind and the rain. Then, it was discovered by a young courting couple. News quickly spread and it became a place for teenagers to meet away from their parent's disapproving eyes. The floor became littered with empty beer bottles, used condoms and two forgotten dog toys tucked into a corner.

CHAPTER 7
JACK

Fluffy was a survivor. He returned to the bungalow a couple of times to scavenge any food left around, but he quickly lost interest. There wasn't a lot there, and his thick coat kept him warm on the coldest days. He didn't require any shelter.

Within a few days, he had adapted to life in the wild. He killed rabbits and small animals and drank from the stream. It was four months before he encountered another human. His white coat was still immaculate. He didn't look like a wild dog.

Jack was a farmer, but he loved to fish, and today, he decided to try to find a more remote spot to try his luck. He wanted a day of undisturbed fishing. Away from people who always asked, "Caught anything?" Then, he was expected to engage in conversation about what time he'd started, which method he was using and how often he came there. The more irritating folk gave advice. "You'd be better with worms. You should fish on the top." Jack was too polite to tell them to 'Bugger off,' but that's what he was thinking. Sometimes, he really, really, really wanted to throw them in.

It was a pleasant day. Perhaps a bit cold, but the sun was showing through andsi warming the ground, so he wandered up to the fork in the river, left the path and followed the stream. He found the perfect spot. The stream ran into a broader, deeper area resembling a lake but with a slight flow. Trees surrounded it with low branches. It's not easy fishing but ideal for fish to hide under the branches and, best, no one in sight. No people. Just the sounds of the birds and the breeze in the trees.

In fact, it had been quite a trek to find this hidden gem, so Jack felt confident that he would be alone for the day. As he settled and began to fish, he became aware of a large white dog looking at him from the side of the stream. It was odd to see such a beautiful dog alone. Jack felt sure someone must be close, but he couldn't hear anyone.

The dog looked at him as if he were deciding what to do. Then, he wandered out of the stream and positioned himself next to Jack. Jack thought about moving. The dog's owner was bound to be around. But the spot was perfect and Jack couldn't see anyone. So he set up his second fishing rod, expecting the dog to wander off.

It didn't.

After an hour or so, Jack's mind began to wander. *What on earth was such a handsome dog doing here in the middle of nowhere?* Jack didn't know of any houses for miles around. In the end, he decided that the dog must have been dumped. Then he spotted a tag on his collar.

He turned the tag over, expecting to find an address or phone number, but it simply said *Fluffy*.

"So, your name's Fluffy, is it?"

Jack smiled to himself. "Bloody Fluffy."

He didn't look very fluffy. In fact, it seemed almost an insult to call this elegant, handsome animal Fluffy.

"You should go off home, Fluffy."

Jack took his sandwich out of his bag. As he unwrapped it, Fluffy licked his lips, staring at Jack's sandwich, expecting a share. "Bloody hell. Now you want my dinner."

Fluffy's loving eyes seemed to look into Jack's and Jack's resolve melted. He tore a bit from his sandwich and offered it to the dog. He expected Fluffy to snatch, but Fluffy took it gently taking care that his teeth didn't touch Jack's fingers. Jack was so taken with the dog that he gave him more than half his lunch and afternoon biscuits. Fluffy sat quietly by

Jack's side all day, only moving when he wanted to pee but returning immediately to him.

As the evening came, Jack started to pack his fishing tackle and head back to his landrover.

"Well, off you go, mate," he said, patting Fluffy on the head. "You need to go home now." But as Jack started to walk, Fluffy followed.

"*Shoo!*" Jack shouted, waving his hand.

Fluffy sat, but as soon as Jack moved, Fluffy was on his feet again. "This is not what I need," Jack told himself. He decided that if Fluffy were still with him when he returned to the car, he would ask around. Someone must know where he came from. He was in such good condition. He couldn't be a stray.

Jack reached the car park. Two other fishermen were there packing their tackle into the back of their vehicles. "Excuse me, mate," said Jack to either of them. "This dog's been following me around all day. Looks in pretty good nick, so he must have a home around here somewhere. I don't suppose you've got any ideas, have you?"

The first fisherman grinned, "Never seen him before, but looks like you've found a friend." He got into his van and drove off.

The second man hesitated, "Handsome looking dog, but no, I haven't seen him before. I live just down in the town. I'm sure I would have noticed a dog like that. Perhaps someone dumped him."

Jack looked at Fluffy. That did seem to be the most obvious explanation. "Thing is…" said Jack, hopefully. I've already got three dogs at home. "Can't really take this one, too."

"There's a kennel just the other side of the village. They take strays. They're okay, nice folk. You could probably take him there in the morning."

"I don't suppose you could take him," said Jack hopefully.

"Sorry, mate," said the fisherman, closing his door. "My misses would kill me if I brought a dog home."

And with that, he was gone. Jack looked at Fluffy. He could just leave him. It wasn't his problem. But Fluffy's eyes looked at Jack with such a sorrowful expression. Jack felt guilty even thinking about leaving him. "Okay, come on, then. But it's kennels first thing in the morning."

Fluffy jumped into the front seat, wagging his tail. He sat looking out of the window as if he belonged there and this was a regular event.

"Bloody hell!" grumbled Jack. "You ate my lunch and now you're acting like you own my car. I'm telling you now, this is temporary. You're not staying." Jack needed to say it out loud so that he could convince himself. Fluffy was going to the kennel first thing in the morning.

A Protected Killer

Jack did indeed have three dogs. But they were three working dogs living in the barn close to the house. They slept on the warm hay, snuggled together. The barn door was always ajar, and they enjoyed the freedom of wandering around the yard and playing together.

In the summer, when Jack left his house door open, the dogs never attempted to come in. They would howl if the barn door were closed. People had said it wasn't right to keep a dog outside, but these dogs never wanted the restrictions of a closed door, so they were happy in the barn. They were working dogs, highly trained Border Collies, which helped Jack herd the sheep. The youngest was born on the farm. He was the pup of Jack's oldest dog, Jess and a planned mating with a champion sheepdog. Although he was young, he showed progress within no time. He was a bit excitable and sometimes scattered the sheep, but Jack recognised this was just enthusiasm. Clive, the young Collie, was doing well. The other dog was a middle-aged dog called Rex. Jack had bought

Rex as a puppy and trained him himself. Rex was an honest and hardworking worker and had never let Jack down. He would work until he was exhausted. On a hot day, Rex would run for hours and then take himself for a swim in the lake. The lake was manmade or to be more precise, Jack made it. Jack had hoped to stock the lake with carp, but that never happened. Jack reasoned that catching the same fish in the same place would probably be boring. The lake was a useful water source in dry weather, so it was left. It became a haven for wildlife and a swimming pool for Jack's dogs when they returned from work on a warm day.

Jack had been brought up on the farm. His father was a farmer and his grandfather before him. Jack had never considered doing anything else. Jack remembered his childhood on this farm being carefree and happy. His mother in the kitchen would produce wonderful meals. The smell of homemade cooking from the kitchen drifted across the farmyard and the memory would still make Jack's stomach rumble.

His father worked hard and as Jack got older, his father would take Jack with him. Jack could sheer a sheep before he was ten. Jack was a runner-up in the junior sheep dog trials and helped to train and look after the farm dogs.

Those were carefree days, and Jack couldn't recall any talk about finances. He knew they weren't rich. He didn't seem to have the expensive toys that his school friends had, but Jack had other things. His school friends were envious of Jack being able not just to ride but drive a real tractor. His friends would visit often, preferring to climb trees and feed the baby lambs rather than play with the expensive toys purchased by their parents. He was a popular and intelligent lad who caught the eye of many of the young girls. He had his first kiss behind the barn with Mary Jane when they were both fifteen. He thought he was in love until he met Carol.

Carol showed him that life could be more than kisses, but she moved with her parents into the city, and Jack never saw her again.

Jack felt shy in female company. His life on the farm didn't give him much opportunity to meet women and Jack didn't think much about them. He was content and busy on the farm.

He was twenty-three when his father died suddenly of a heart attack. His mother was ageing and seemed unable to cope with the loss. She spent most of her time sitting in the kitchen. It was then that Jack realised how much farming had changed. He became aware that general living costs were rising disproportionately to his income. He spent many evenings pondering over the books and trying to work out how he could afford to manage the farm in the long term. When he finally admitted that his mother couldn't safely be left on her own all day, he reluctantly moved her into a local nursing home. She was happy, but the bills were more than Jack could afford.

Jack was no fool. He could have given up the farm, but he decided to diversify. He laid one of the fields to grassland. Jack's family had farmhands who lived on site, but Jack decided to pull some caravans onto the bottom field. He only hired temporary staff when he needed them. He didn't have to pay a regular wage bill.

He refurbished the old farm labourers cottage and let it to a lady with two children. Jack had been apprehensive at first. He would have preferred a childless couple. He was concerned that the children, coming from a city, would be unaware of the dangers of their new surroundings, particularly when he realised that the youngest girl had Down Syndrome.

But the mother, Katherine, seemed desperate and promised that the children wouldn't interfere. Jack had fenced a small area around the cottage for a garden so the children would have no reason to venture into the farm yard. Katherine's references were excellent and Jack was keen to let the property and begin to realise the income, so the tenancy was signed and Katherine moved in.

That was eighteen months ago. Jack certainly had no regrets. Katherine was more like a friend than a tenant.

When Jack had been working all day on the farm, he returned to find a basket on his doorstep containing a homemade apple pie. As he lifted the cover, the smell brought back beautiful memories of his mother in the kitchen. It brought a tear to Jack's eye.

Katherine would frequently invite Jack in for tea and there were always homemade biscuits or cakes to accompany the tea.

Katherine struggled but always paid her rent. In lambing season or if Jack was ever short on temporary labour,

Katherine was only too willing to join the workforce, often being a lifeline to Jack.

Katherine was strong and took quickly to lambing and landwork. She reminded Jack, so much of a younger version of his mother. At first glance, Katherine seemed like a plain-looking woman, but she had curly hair that bounced as she moved. Perhaps a little plump but flawless skin and dark sparkling eyes. Her face seemed to light up when she smiled and Jack had to admit he was secretly in love.

Katherine had left her husband when he had refused to give up his mistress. Jack believed that Katherine had no desire to begin another relationship.

Jack kept his feelings to himself, not wanting to jeopodise their friendship and recognising the business arrangement. But it didn't stop him from dreaming about Katherine at night or worrying when he didn't see her for a day. He had once knocked on her door to ask if she was okay, but afterward, Jack was worried that he had overstepped the mark and felt that his actions were stupid and interfering.

Two months ago, Jack's mother had passed away. Katherine had comforted Jack and cooked for him for a whole week, telling him he must eat. She had accompanied Jack to the funeral and held his hand. When the ashes were scattered in the same place as his father's ashes, Katherine was there. She was a friend, and although Jack dreamed of something more, there was no way to move forward.

Most of the time, Katherine was true to her word and kept the children away from the farmyard, but Molly, Katherine's seven-year-old, tended to wander when Katherine visited the farm.

They all knew where she would be. Down Syndrom children are known to be very affectionate and Molly was no exception. She always wanted to cuddle the sheep or play with the dogs. Her brother Michael often came running to find Jack and Katherine to report that Molly was in the barn with the dogs and wouldn't come out.

Jack didn't really mind; instead, he couldn't help feeling affection for her. He allowed her to feed any orphaned lambs. A task that Molly loved. On one occasion, they caught Molly with a bottle of milk, trying to feed a full-grown sheep. They had to try to explain to Molly that only some of the lambs needed to be hand-fed and big sheep didn't like milk from the milkman.

The dogs weren't keen on anyone, not even Molly. They wagged their tails when Jack petted them and always came when called. But they were working dogs, not pets. Although not aggressive when Molly tried to stroke them, they simply moved away.

Molly would often chase them, saying, "Come for a cuddle," but there was plenty of room for the dogs to disappear until Molly found something else to amuse her.

She talked to the butterflies, loved the lambs and rescued flies from the water trough.

"Leave those poor dogs alone," Katherine would scold Molly when Molly chased them around.

Molly loved everything and everyone and believed that the more love she gave, the more love she would get back. So when the dogs showed no interest in her, she gave them presents. She drew them pictures and left them in the barn. And she tried to fluff up the hay to make their bed more comfortable.

When Jack returned from his fishing trip with his newfound friend, Fluffy, his first thought was to put him in the barn with the other dogs, but as Jack opened the barn door, all three dogs began to growl. Clearly, they'd taken an instant dislike to Fluffy.

"Oh well!" said Jack, resigned to the issues his new visitor was causing. "Looks like you'll have to come in the house, but it's only for one night. Tomorrow, you're off to the kennels."

Fluffy curled up in front of the fire and slept. He had a full belly, and the warm crackling of the fire made the setting peaceful. The glow glimmered on Fluffy's white coat. Jack sat with his legs crossed, thinking about what a wonderful painting the scene would be. He dozed contentedly and dreamt of Katherine. When Jack rose the next morning, Fluffy was sat by the door.

"So you're house-trained, too," said Jack with a smile. He took an old lead from the coat hanger by the door. He couldn't remember the last time it had been used. His other dogs didn't need leads. They would jump onto the trailer when Jack set off to work. They never left the farm.

Jack put Fluffy on the lead and couldn't resist heading past Katherine's cottage toward the bottom field. As he walked through the yard, Jack's older dog spotted Fluffy and immediately began to growl. Jack quickly walked on. Katherine spotted Jack through the window and came running out of the cottage. "Good morning," she said, smiling. "And who's this?'

"His name's Fluffy. I found him when I was fishing yesterday. Couldn't get rid of him, but I'm going to take him to the kennel a bit later. I can't keep him."

Katherine looked at Fluffy. "He's certainly a handsome dog."

At that moment, Molly spotted Fluffy and ran towards them. Katherine had accidentally left the door open. Before Katherine had time to stop her, Molly had Fluffy in a full embrace, putting her face right next to Fluffy.

Jack and Katherine gasped and tried to separate them quickly. Both feared Fluffy may not react favourably to being grabbed by a child.

"Fluffy," said Jack, hoping his shout may startle the dog and prevent him from focusing on Molly. But Fluffy turned his enormous face to Molly and gave her a big lick on her cheek.

"Fluffy!" repeated Molly. "Nice doggy."

Both Jack and Katherine smiled at what had just happened. "Cup of tea?" Katherine asked.

Jack never wanted to turn down a cup of tea with Katherine, so he and Fluffy followed her into the cottage and sat at her wooden kitchen table. Jack fetched the wood from the shed for her and lit her fire.

Although weary at first, Jack and Katherine watched as Molly and Michael brought Fluffy a selection of their cuddly toys and played with him. Fluffy seemed to enjoy the attention and made them all laugh when he put one of the teddies into Molly's doll's pushchair.

"He's gorgeous!" said Katherine. "Pity you can't keep him."

"I can't," said Jack flatly. "My other dogs hate him. They're really nasty to him. I'm a bit surprised. I've never seen them behave like that, but I suppose they're an established pack and don't want a newcomer."

"I'd take him myself," said Katherine, "but he's such a big dog and I've got my hands pretty full with the kids." Katherine thought for a while. "But I can look after him when you are busy if that would help."

Jack really didn't want another dog. And certainly not a house dog. His dogs had always lived outside. But as he watched Fluffy playing with the children, he started to wonder if Fluffy might provide a reason for him to see more of Katherine and that was certainly worth any inconvenience. And why not? Fluffy was house-trained and seemed to want no more than a comfy place in front of Jack's fire.

"Well, I suppose I could," said Jack slowly. "But only if you can help. I can't take him to work. I'm not sure how he'd behave around the sheep, and my other dogs won't tolerate him, so I'd have to give him to you when I'm working out in the fields."

"Molly and Michael would love that," Katherine said.

For the next half an hour, Jack and Katherine watched Fluffy and the children play. Fluffy didn't seem to mind anything, even when they tied a baby bonnet around his head and tried to sit him in the child's pushchair. Fluffy was far too big for the pushchair, but he managed to somehow sit on the top until they tried to turn a corner and the whole thing collapsed. Fluffy's head came up from under the blankets, looking like he was wearing a nun's habit.

"That poor dog," said Katherine, but she laughed so much that tears ran down her face. Jack thought she looked more beautiful than ever.

Jack could have left Fluffy with Katherine that day, but he hadn't been fed. He thought about placing a few adverts around town to see if someone had lost a dog, but he decided it was a lot of effort and he had found Fluffy some distance away. If anyone had lost a beloved pet, surely it was up to them to advertise. He felt sure Fluffy had been dumped for some reason. He had mixed feelings. Katherine was clearly taken with Fluffy and Fluffy seemed to be settling quickly. So he resigned himself to the idea that he now had another dog.

He fed Fluffy and prepared to leave for the fields to work. He needed to move some of the sheep from the lower field to a new grazing land. He made himself some sandwiches. His idea was to shut Fluffy in the barn while he was away. He didn't completely trust him in the house on his own all day.

He may not be completely housetrained or may destroy the furniture. He'd be fine in the large barn as long as the other dogs were away. They clearly didn't like Fluffy.

He loaded his lunch into the cab and the dogs into the trailer, then went to fetch Fluffy. But before he had the chance to slip a lead on him, Fluffy shot past Jack and straight into the cab's passenger seat as if he owned it.

Jack looked at him, amused. *Oh well, why not,* thought Jack. It would probably be better if Jack could keep an eye on him. He could close the cab door when they are around the sheep.

The other dogs started growling a low, threatening growl as soon as they saw Fluffy. But Fluffy was a newcomer and clearly not a working dog. So Jack just reasoned that they would come to tolerate his presence even if they weren't going to be friends.

When Jack drove to the field, he expected Fluffy to react to the sheep, barking or jumping around, but Fluffy just sat, showing no reaction.

"You must have seen sheep before," said Jack. He was impressed and thought, *Fluffy clearly wasn't going to be a problem at all.*

Jack closed the cab's door, called his other dogs, and began work. It was a hard day. The dogs worked well, but the sheep were challenging today. When Jack's youngest dog left even a small gap, the sheep took advantage. They just wanted to escape. It took two hours to move the sheep. Jack climbed into his cab and realised that he had left his sandwiches on the dashboard. Fluffy hadn't touched them. Jack unwrapped the sandwiches and offered Fluffy a corner. Fluffy took it in the same gentle way as he had the previous day at the fishing lake.

Jack checked the fences, secured a couple of the posts and headed back to the farm yard. Hot after the day's work, the dogs jumped out of the trailer and headed for the lake. Fluffy seemed to look after them longingly. Jack slipped a lead on Fluffy and followed his dogs to the lake, but as he neared the lake, the dogs lined up at the edge and started growling. They were not going to make friends. Jack would bring Fluffy to the lake later when the dogs settled back in the barn.

Over the next few weeks, Jack saw Katherine on most days. Sometimes, she would take Fluffy to her cottage and particularly enjoyed having him when her children were not at school. The children adored Fluffy and Fluffy never seemed to mind taking part in their games. They made a harness and got Fluffy to pull the doll's pushchair with a doll in it. They often dressed Fluffy in doll clothes, and kissed and cuddled him. Once, when Jack was a bit late coming back from the fields, he was greeted by Katherine withher finger to her lips, "Quiet," she said, smiling. When he entered the living room, Michael, Molly and Fluffy had made a makeshift bed out of dolls blankets and pillows. All three were curled up asleep with three heads on the pillow and bodies covered in blankets. Katherine took a photo.

"I'm tempted to leave them there," said Katherine. "They look so peaceful."

But Molly started to stir, and Fluffy realisng Jack was in the room, slowly got up, stretched and wandered over to Jack's side.

"Come on, Fluffy," Jack said. "Time for home."

Fluffy seemed to understand. He licked Molly's hand as if to say goodbye, and without saying another word, he slipped past Jack through the door and jumped into the waiting landrover.

"See you tomorrow, Fluffy," called Molly sleepily. "I love you."

Jack and Katherine both knew that as a down-syndrome child, Molly was not expected to have a long life. Katherine loved both of her children and was determined not to show any favouritism, but, at the same time, it felt desperately important to her to make Molly's life as happy and fulfilling as possible.

As Katherine looked at her daughter, smiling and waving to Fluffy, a glow of satisfaction and gratitude swept across her face. Molly was truly happy.

Jack looked at the scene and felt that Fluffy had been heaven-sent. This new presence brought something new and rewarding to their lives. Fluffy was what Molly needed. Fluffy was what they all needed.

As Jack had hoped, Katherine became a more frequent visitor to the farmhouse and Jack to the cottage. In fact, some days, Jack would return from a long day at work to find cooking smells emerging from the kitchen. Katherine was treating the farmhouse as an extension of her home. The door was never locked, so Katherine often let herself in and cooked meals for them to eat together. She cleaned the house and even made some new curtains for the parlour.

Jack no longer waited to be invited into Katherine's cottage. He made a polite knock at the door and then walked in. She was always pleased to see him with Fluffy at his side and always seemed to be making tea, which she served with biscuits or homemade cakes.

But although she sometimes gave Jack an affectionate peck on the cheek, something told him that he shouldn't push the relationship too far or too quickly. Once or twice, he reached for her hand, but she pulled away and seemed embarrassed. He knew that he would have to bide his time and hoped that there would come a time when Katherine would give him a sign that she was ready to start a new romantic attachment.

He knew she had been hurt when her husband had been unfaithful. Katherine came from a very ordinary family where loyalty was important. The affair was not only hurtful but a complete shock to Katherine and Jack knew that she would need time to put it behind her and move on. But Fluffy seemed to be helping. Certainly, the bond between Katherine and Jack was stronger and more unbreakable now than ever.

The children seemed to lead an ideal life and were very happy, which made Katherine happy. She commented that the move into the cottage was the best decision she had ever made. Her remark filled Jack's heart with a warm glow.

Molly attended a special school and was doing well. She took part in a school concert which Jack, Katherine and Michael attended and they all felt a sense of pride watching as Molly sang her heart out at the front of the stage. After the concert, Molly ran over to them, shouting, "Did you love me singing?" She was, as always, full of love. She would often say she loved things or people, but to Molly, love wasn't just a word. She really did love everything and needed to feel the same love in return.

It certainly wasn't difficult to love Molly. If anyone looked sad, Molly would fetch them a tissue and give them a hug. Fluffy, too, would sense unhappiness and accompany Molly on her venture to cheer people.

Once, when Michael had an argument at school, he came home miserable and grumpy. He sat on the sofa, refusing to talk to anyone. Molly collected the box of tissues from the bathroom, presented them to Michael and hugged him. Fluffy sat on the other side and offered Michael his paw.

Katherine and Jack looked on. "Here come the samaritans," Katherine said quietly to Jack. They both smiled as Michael accepted Fluffy's paw and hugged Molly back with tears in his eyes.

Michael loved the farm. Jack started taking him out when he went to work with the flock. Michael was developing a knack for controlling the dogs and was already able to send them left and right. The younger dog was learning fast and Jack thought he might give the dog to Michael. He hoped Michael might follow in his footsteps and be good enough to enter the junior sheepdog trials.

Michael began to show interest in farm machines and driving the tractors. He learned the functional tips to operate them, but Michael was small for his age and couldn't easily reach the controls. *It will come,* thought Jack. He had a real attachment with Michael and enjoyed teaching him. Michael was always keen to learn and impressed Jack with how quickly he would master such complicated tasks.

Jack remembered when he had taught Michael how to command the dogs. Michael couldn't whistle. Katherine told Jack he had woken her up numerous times in the night practicing how to whistle. In the end, she had to threaten to ban him from the farm for two days unless he stopped and let her get some sleep.

Michael was bright but didn't do well at school. Katherine was summoned to the school one day because Michael had told his teacher he didn't need to do maths because he wanted to be a farmer. Jack had to explain to Michael that farming also involved paperwork. Jack started showing Michael how to document sheep movements and calculate orders for animal feed. Michael's maths and writing skills improved almost overnight.

Jack was happier than he had ever been. There was just one thing missing from his life. No matter what happened during the day, happy days sharing picnics in the cottage garden, lazy days strolling with Fluffy and the children or evenings by a fire sharing a bottle of wine, Katherine always went to her own bed and Jack retired for the night alone to dream of the night when he could reach out and find Katherine next to him instead of the warm mass of fur that was Fluffy. Jack dreamed of Katherine every night. Sometimes, even in the day, his mind would wander to thoughts of her. He longed to be close to her, feel her warmth, and smell that sweet smell of her hair that teased him as she passed. He wanted to wrap his arms around her and breathe her in. His body felt empty and the pain felt so intense he thought it would eat him inside. He had nightmares that one day she would be snatched by another man. Jack would wake up with an electric jolt in his body and sweat pouring off his brows. He'd move into the corner of the bed and shiver. But he was not sure if it was fear. Longing? Heartbreak? He knew only two things, that he couldn't be without Katherine in his life, but he also needed to make the most of every second with her, just in case…

It was the first week of September. The end of the most beautiful summer. It was Michael's first day back at school and the start of the new term. Molly's school term was due to start a week later, so Katherine strolled up to the farmhouse. Jack had planned to do paperwork. He had invoices to settle and orders to place, but when he heard the latch on the kitchen door open, he dropped all thoughts of the paperwork and joined Katherine and Molly in the kitchen for morning coffee.

Katherine, Jack thought, *looked more lovely than ever.* She was wearing the floral dress that Jack loved. Although Katherine wasn't slim, she still had an hourglass shape and the dress showed her figure.

As they sat drinking coffee, Molly wandered into the yard with Fluffy. Molly was throwing a stick for Fluffy and giggling as Fluffy dropped it at her feet. They silently watched her through the window, smiling at Molly's sheer delight.

Suddenly, Jack was overcome. His feelings of love felt all-consuming. At that moment, there was nothing else. As they watched Molly playing, Jack thought his life was nearly perfect. He reached for Katherine's hand. "You're beautiful," he whispered. He had expected her to pull away, to make a joke, or to tell him he was being silly, but she left her hand in his.

After a while, she looked up into his eyes and whispered, "I think I love you, Jack."

Jack's mind exploded. Had he heard that, right? Was his mind playing a cruel trick? Did she really just say that?

"Say it again. Please say it again. Please let me hear what you said, say it again."

She smiled. The twinkle in those dark eyes melted his heart and she said, "I love you, Jack."

The pent-up feelings that Jack had harboured for so long were released at that moment. He leapt from his chair and took her in his arms. She tilted her face and kissed him on the lips. Jack needed her so much. He was wrapped in the taste of her, the smell of her.

"Where's Molly?" she said anxiously.

"It's okay, she's just outside with Fluffy. She's playing. I can see her. She's fine," Jack replied, his heart full of love. *There can be no stoping at this point,* he thought, and they sunk to the floor.

It all happened so quickly. Molly threw the stick. It bounced off the wall and into the barn. The other dogs were in the barn and Molly knew they didn't like to play, but she loved them too. She loved all the dogs. Fluffy didn't fetch the stick, so Molly went to fetch it. As Molly was picking up the stick, she heard the dogs growling. She looked behind her and Fluffy had followed her. He stared at the growling dogs. Molly turned to the dogs and scolded them, "Naughty dogs." But the dogs were focused on Fluffy. "You should be nice to

Fluffy," said Molly, picking up the stick. But Fluffy didn't look nice. His ears had flattened against his head and his face had changed to a scowling beast. As he charged forward, Molly thought he was going to fight the other dogs. She moved to bar the way, but Fluffy leapt at her, pushing her to the floor and tearing her throat apart. Fluffy was a strong dog. It took him a few minutes to rip out her throat, then he dragged her by the foot, biting so hard that her foot was ripped from her motionless leg. He grabbed at her face and shook until pieces of flesh were torn away. Still not sated, he bit hard onto the hand he had just that morning licked so affectionately.

It was over for Molly quite quickly. The bite to her throat had cut off her trachea, but Fluffy continued his attack. After a few minutes of tearing Molly's lifeless body into pieces, he seemed to lose interest. He was hot and headed for the lake to cool down.

The other dogs watched him attacking poor Molly in shock, but now curious, they approached Molly's lifeless body. They pawed at it, sniffed at it, circled it, unsure of what to do.

Jack and Katherine stood still, embracing as Katherine rearranged her disheveled clothing. As she kissed Jack, she glanced through the window. "Where's Molly?" she asked. Katherine had a sense of panic as she rushed to the door shouting, "Molly where are you?"

"She won't have gone far," shouted Jack after her. "She was there just a few minutes ago."

It was true, she had been there just a few minutes before. Jack had been so eager to take Katherine. It was a fevered, almost animal attempt at lovemaking. Jack tried so hard to be gentle and patient, but he had wanted her for so long. And she had responded to him in the same way. He was surprised and grateful that she seemed to feel as he did. There would be time later for a different, gentle approach. For now, they both needed to satisfy a need.

The barn was the only place to start to look at. It was close to the house, although Molly had shown less interest in the other dogs now that she had Fluffy. However, Molly loved all animals, so she would often wander into the barn to say "Hello" to the dogs.

Katherine threw the barn door wide open. For a moment, she seemed as if she couldn't quite comprehend the horrific scene in front of her. As Jack caught her up and looked into the barn, he couldn't believe his eyes. Katherine then started to scream. The most ear-piercing scream Jack had ever heard.

Everything became a blur. Slow motion. Like a dream that was a nightmare. Jack pulled Katherine outside. She sat crumpled on the floor sobbing. There were no words. Jack couldn't find words. He left her on the floor, went back into the house and phoned the police. He could never remember what he said. Then he got his gun. Without hesitation, he went back to the barn, passing the sobbing, crumpled heap that was Katherine. Three shots rang out. He had shot all three dogs. They would never hurt anyone ever again.

Fluffy had swum in the lake, and because of the chaos, he had returned to the house unnoticed. It was a warm day and he had dried quickly. He lay quietly in the corner of the kitchen as the chaos of police and people in white suits charged around the farm. Fluffy's white fur gleamed.

Jack sat on the kitchen chair with his head in his hands, sobbing. He had vomited down the front of his shirt. A police officer sat in front of him, but Jack was not able to talk.

It seemed like hours before Jack was able to lift his head and speak. He looked at the man in front of him. Obviously, police but in plain clothes.

"Where's Katherine? I need to go to Katherine."

The man looked at Jack. "I'm sorry, but she doesn't want to see you or anyone else."

"But you don't understand," said Jack. He guessed they thought Katherine was just his tenant. Jack thought they would take him to her once he told them that he loved her, that she loved him. He needed to be with her.

"She's moving out immediately," said the man. "I'm sure you understand, but she doesn't want to be here. She's getting her things together as we speak. But she did ask me to give you this," he passed an envelope.

Jack snatched at it, ripping it open expecting a note, something to say she'd be in contact, something to tell him what to do, where to go, anything. But when he opened the envelope, there was a small pile of crisp ten-pound notes—this month's rent.

Over the next few weeks, Jack couldn't eat. He drank all the wine he had, then ordered more. The sheep remained in the bottom field unattended. Invoices weren't paid and his answer machine was full of suppliers asking for money.

Fluffy never left his side but Jack had a sick feeling every time he looked at him. He knew Fluffy had nothing to do with the attack. Fluffy must have returned to the house at some point, but he had no blood or marks, so he couldn't have been around when the dogs attacked Molly.

He guessed that Molly, finding herself alone, had wandered into the barn. Perhaps she had cornered the dogs and tried to cuddle them. But whatever had happened, Fluffy was a dog and Jack couldn't stand dogs.

With a heavy heart, he took Fluffy to the rehoming kennel. Josy, the kennel maid, saw a frail, sick man—a broken man with a beautiful white dog. Josy looked at Jack and didn't feel that she could ask questions.

"Yes, of course, we'll take him," said Josy

"I can't take care of him," said Jack, tears streaming down his face. "I can't…" he couldn't even finish the words. He turned and shuffled away.

CHAPTER 8
MICHELLE AND NUMAN

It had been nearly three years since the horrific attack which killed Michelle's baby and left the pretty young mum unrecognisable. She was so disfigured that most people turned their heads, unable to look at her.

Numerous operations, skin grafts and procedures had done little to improve her appearance. A skin graft had rejected, an infection had set in, and although surgeons had tried to take skin from her thighs and buttocks, there was just too much tissue and skin missing. Her teeth and gums were still exposed on one side, and her cheek was completely missing. Attempts to replace the missing eye were near to impossible because her eye socket had been damaged, so when she tried to wear the false eye, it caused her pain and sometimes fell out.

She, at last, gave up and only left her mum's flat for medical appointments. Even on those trips, she wore her thick black veil. She didn't want to see the horrified faces of strangers as they turned away. She couldn't even look at herself. She insisted all the mirrors in her mum's flat were removed along with the photos of her before the attack. She couldn't bear to look at them.

She was moody and depressed. Sometimes, she wondered if she should take her life, but she still felt an overwhelming desire to know what happened to the white dog. She couldn't rest until she knew for sure that it was dead. She reasoned that the dog would die of old age, so perhaps in a few more years, she could find some comfort.

Perhaps then she could take her life or what was left of it. Numan continued to visit Michelle and he had promised he would never give up in trying to find the dog responsible for Michelle's injuries. He had reinterviewed Chris, the homeless drunken man who said he had tied the dog to the gate of the rehoming centre. Still, Numan suspected Chris wasn't telling him the whole truth. Although he had kept Chris in police cells in an attempt to make him sober enough to recall the incident, Chris had never given any additional information. He had reinterviewed Mick, too—the homeless man who had first tipped Numan off about the white dog. For another twenty pounds, Mick had suddenly recalled that the dog's name was Duffy or Roughy, something like that. Numan took an interest in dog attacks throughout the country in a vague hope that the white dog may surface again somewhere.

Over a period of time, Numan began to get a reputation for being quite an authority figure on dog attacks. Other police forces would contact Numan for help and advice. It was then that Numan was able to secure funding to offer

Michelle some part-time work to do research on dog attacks. Numan quickly realised that people would go to any lengths to protect their vicious animals. There was always an excuse, "It wasn't my dog" or "He was provoked." When asked if the police could see the dog, it usually disappeared without a trace. "I gave it away, but I can't remember who I gave it to," or "It died."

Michelle had nothing better to do and was pleased to have something valuable to occupy her mind. When a dog had bitten someone and disappeared, Michelle would search through social media pages for details about the owner, their family and friends in an attempt to find who was likely to be hiding the dog.

She'd been fairly successful, often coming up with a name, address and even photos of the dog in question.

Numan knew she liked dark chocolate and would often bring a bar when he visited. At Easter he ordered a special enormous dark chocolate easter egg. She laughed when she saw it and said, "I hope this doesn't mean you're not going to visit for a year."

Numan still struggled with Michelle's appearance. Although he saw her regularly, each time seemed like a new shock. He couldn't believe how she had survived and sometimes wondered if she would have been better dying that day. He didn't turn his head away and tried his best to treat her as a normal human being. Whenever she tried eating the chocolate, she would post it into the gap in her teeth, dribble brown saliva down her front, and rasp as she attempted to breathe while eating. It wasn't easy to concentrate on anything other than Michelle's disgusting appearance.

Then, one day, Numan was told about a dog attack at a farm. It caught his eye because it was in the same district as the rehoming centre where Chris had claimed to have tied up the white dog. But when Numan looked more closely at the case, the dogs were three Border Collies. A phone call confirmed the details of the tragic case and that all three dogs had been shot by the farmer who owned them.

Numan put the details into his filing tray but kept going back to it, reading and re-reading the details. Something kept nagging at him. He had become interested in why dogs attack. *No such thing as a bad dog, just a bad owner,* people told him. Often, that seemed to be true, but these dogs were working dogs that worked around sheep. They weren't the sort of dogs that would chase animals or children and Numan hadn't come across many vicious border collies. He left the file on his desk and decided that when things had settled, he could visit the farmer at some point. He hoped that the farmer would help him understand what had happened. Had the dogs shown any sign of aggression before? What about their parentage?

Numan hoped that one day, someone would work it all out so that attacks would become more predictable and consequently more preventable. He didn't mention the attack to Michelle. There was no point. The area was a coincidence. The dogs were Collies and anyway, they were dead.

CHAPTER 9
MARIE'S STORY

Josy stared down at the beautiful white dog. He looked up at her, wagging his tail.

He was a full-grown, large dog. Josy guessed he was about six or seven. She would have liked to have gotten more details from the man, but his obvious distress made Josy reluctant to ask questions.

Yet again, the kennels were full. She'd have to double them up again. She completed the record quickly to book the dog into the centre. The dog sat next to her quietly while she completed the paperwork. *Well behaved,* she thought. *And handsome.* He would probably be rehomed quite quickly. She noticed a disc on his collar. It was slightly worn but said quite clearly, 'Fluffy.' She entered it into the record and proceeded to take Fluffy to the pens.

She was still wondering where to put Fluffy. The phone was ringing, and she needed to call volunteer dog walkers. Fluffy stopped next to a pen with a German shepherd in it. Both dogs greeted each other, wagging their tails. They were a similar size and appeared to like each other. Josy opened the pen and Fluffy ran in. Josy watched for a moment, but there were no signs of aggression, so she hurried off to perform her other duties.

It was much later in the day when she realised her mistake. The German Shepherd was called Bella—a bitch. *Oops!* She'd have to find another pen for Fluffy. When she went to retrieve Fluffy, both dogs were lying down together in the corner. They didn't look particularly amorous, and Josy didn't think Bella was on heat. She breathed a sigh of relief and retrieved Fluffy from the pen. But what now? She still had to find somewhere to put him.

Marie was a volunteer dog walker and Josy's auntie. Marie lived in the town and enjoyed coming to help walk the dogs. It was good exercise and away from the noise and traffic. Marie liked dogs, but she was a part-time childminder, and she said she hadn't got time or space to adopt a dog, although Josy was always trying to persuade her.

Josy often showed Marie, another cute dog, with a sad story, but Marie was adamant. She was happy to help by walking the dogs and fundraising for them. She had even once run the kennels for a week when Josy took a holiday. But she drew the line at taking a dog permanently.

A young couple had visited the kennel earlier in the day. They were particularly interested in a young greyhound with clipped ears. They expressed disgust at how cruel people could be to animals. They stroked the dog affectionately. Josy had agreed that they could take the dog, but it had to be subject to background checks and veterinary examinations to identify any health issues before it could be rehomed.

On the same day, an elderly lady visited and fell in love with an aging Yorkshire terrier with very few teeth. Josy was thrilled. She had thought she might have difficulty homing the dog, which was clearly in his last years of life.

That was life in the kennel. It came in waves. One day, the kennels would be full to overflowing and the next potential owners would arrive almost as if there had been a coach party, and the kennels would be emptied. So Josy knew that in a few weeks, there would be space. She just had a problem right now.

"It's just a foster arrangement," pleaded Josy on the phone. "He's gorgeous and it's only for a few weeks."

Marie was adamant. "No, Josy. I told you I'm happy to help with most things, but I don't want a dog in my house. It's not big enough," Marie insisted.

"I've got kids' toys all over the place. It will mess in the garden where the kids play and when I'm childminding, I can't take it out for a walk. It's too much responsibility!"

Josy sighed. Then her voice cracked as the sad realisation and truth dawned on her. "Auntie Marie," she sobbed. "I think I'm going to have to put one of the dogs to sleep. I've never had to do it before, but most of the pens are doubled at the moment. I know they're going to be spare kennels as soon as I can get the checks done and the dogs out, but it's going to take time and I'm trying to run this place almost single-handedly. The other kennel maid is sick again. I don't know what to do."

Marie hesitated.

Josy heard the intake of breath and tried one last time. "If you take him. I'll promise I'll take him back in three weeks no matter what. And on the days when you're childminding, I'll come round after work and walk him myself. Please, Auntie Marie. I can't face killing one of the dogs. I've always been able to rehome them. It's just a time thing."

Marie sighed. She knew how it would break Josy's heart to destroy a healthy dog.

Once a dog had come to the kennel severely malnourished, Josy had slept at the kennel trying to feed the dog small amounts of food throughout the day and night. She had tried for five days, but the dog was too far gone. It died in its sleep on the fifth day and Josy cried for a whole month afterward.

"Okay, Josy, but it's three weeks and that's it! If you don't pick him up after three weeks, I'll take him to the vet myself. And this is a one-off. Don't ask again."

"Thank you, thank you, thank you," said Josy. "You won't regret it. He's gorgeous and really well-behaved. You'll hardly notice he's there."

"Don't push it, Josy!" warned Marie. "Three weeks and that's it!"

"I'll drop him around after work," Josy replied, sniffing. She then ended the call and wiped away her tears.

***

Josy looked at Fluffy. He wagged his tail. Of course the reality was it would be unlikely that Fluffy would have been the chosen sacrifice. If it really had come to that Josy would have had to have selected one of the dogs which were less desirable and more difficult to home. But Fluffy was last in, so would that decision have been fair?

Thankfully it wasn't something she had to ponder now. The problem was solved. She looked down at Fluffy, "You are a very handsome lad, but you're also a very lucky lad. Luckier than you can possibly know."

Josy dropped Fluffy off just after five that evening. Marie had to agree that he was completely adorable. Fluffy wagged his tail every time Marie spoke to him and seemed so gentle. He didn't snatch when she offered him a biscuit and sat by the door when he needed to go outside. He came when called and even offered Marie his paw when asked.

"How is he around children?" Marie asked.

Josy had to admit that she didn't know, but she couldn't see any problems. He was so gentle. At best, he would be great with children. At worst, he would just ignore them, but he didn't show any sign of aggression and seemed to be a very obedient dog. Josy suggested if Marie was at all concerned that she could simply commanded him to sit and stay.

Josy had been amazed earlier in the day when Fluffy not only obeyed commands, but she was able to tell him to stay, walk away, out of sight, and when she returned, Fluffy was in the exact same spot. He hadn't moved a muscle. *Someone must have trained this dog really well,* she thought.

Even so, Marie was sticking to her guns and reminded Josy several times that this was for three weeks only.

When Josy left, Marie eyed Fluffy. He was a very handsome dog. He wandered over to the toy box in the corner, nosed in the box and came out with a bright yellow teddy. He carried it over to Marie, then sat curled up next to her with his teddy.

"So you've picked yourself a toy," Marie smiled. "You are such a cute dog."

Fluffy wagged his tail.

"But you're not staying," Marie said, just to confirm the point.

The next morning was Tuesday. Tuesday was the day Marie looked after Kevin and Patrick. Marie looked after them every Tuesday, then a little girl aged three and her four-month-old baby sister on a Thursday and Saturday.

Keven and Patrick were the most challenging. Two very noisy brothers aged four and five. Kevin, the oldest, recently started school just around the corner from Marie's house. Although Marie was an experienced childminder, she sometimes wondered if she could actually cope if both boys were at home all day.

They used to go to a nursery in the town, but their behaviour had been described as challenging so the nursery had said they didn't think they were ready for a nursery place. They said they would be better off at home or with a childminder where they could get more individual attention.

Marie didn't believe any child from such a nice family could be that bad, so she agreed to take them once a week to give their mother a break and an opportunity to shop and do whatever she wanted to do. A chance to relax while the boy's father was at work.

But Marie was concerned that the first time Fluffy was going to meet children in her care, it would be the two boys. They were extremely boisterous and loud. Marie always checked before they arrived that anything breakable or dangerous was removed from the room. They weren't really naughty, but they didn't seem to have boundaries. They would search cupboards for something to play with, draw on any paper that was lying around, including important letters, turn all of the furniture into their den, upend the coffee table, and use the curtains to provide a 'roof' over the armchair.

The house was always in chaos within five minutes of their arrival—and the noise. They would howl with laughter, but it seemed like they were permanently attached to a loudspeaker.

Marie tried to read them stories but they weren't interested, preferring more boisterous play. For the few hours that Kevin was at school things were slightly calmer, but only slightly. Even on his own, Patrick would find the noisiest way possible to amuse himself, playing drums, shouting at the TV or singing very loudly.

That morning, the boys were a little late arriving so Marie had to leave to drop Kevin at school almost straight away. She gathered the boys together quickly and put their coats on. She was about to leave when Fluffy appeared carrying his lead.

"A doggie!" said Patrick excitedly.

Marie positioned herself between the boys and Fluffy.

"You mustn't touch him," warned Marie. "He's probably not used to children, and you don't want to frighten him."

Marie wasn't sure whether to take Fluffy on the walk to the school but she reasoned that he seemed well behaved.

Josy had told her how he walked to heel and didn't pull on a lead. It also meant that he would have a walk that day, even if it were a short one. She suspected that Josy might get 'tied up at work' and not arrive to take Fluffy out. So she cautiously put Fluffy's lead on and walked outside with the boys.

Fluffy behaved impeccably. He walked to heel, wagging his tail and didn't falter even when they got close to the school gates, where there were large groups of noisy children.

A few people stopped Marie to comment on the handsome dog. Marie was tempted to say he was looking for a home, but she hadn't had a chance to get to know Fluffy, so she was reluctant to get involved in selecting a suitable home. Best leave that to Josy!

Marie was cautious when she returned home with Fluffy and Patrick. She didn't want to leave them alone together for a second, not even to make a cup of tea. But Patrick was insistent that he wanted to pat the doggie, so Marie allowed him to approach Fluffy as long as he was quiet and gentle.

Fluffy rewarded Patrick's attention with a big lick. Marie was still apprehensive, but as the day wore on, she began to relax. Fluffy seemed to have a calming influence on Patrick. Patrick sat talking and singing to Fluffy in a quiet voice. When Marie announced that they needed to prepare lunch, Patrick scolded Marie, saying, "Don't shout. You'll frighten Fluffy."

When Marie placed Patrick's lunch in front of him, she was again on full alert. Dogs could be unpredictable around food, but she didn't need to worry about it. Fluffy sat by Patrick making no effort to take his food, until Patrick broke a bit off his biscuit and offered it to Fluffy. Fluffy took it gently from his fingers, making sure his teeth didn't come into contact with Patrick's skin.

Marie thought, *Fluffy must have been a well-trained family dog.*

Later that day, they collected Kevin from school. Marie watched in disbelief as both boys sat quietly, stroking Fluffy, talking quietly and playing teddy bear's picnic with Fluffy's yellow bear and two more from the toy box.

When it was time for the boys to leave, they didn't want to go home. They kissed Fluffy on his nose and told him they'd come to play with him again soon. Fluffy raised his paw, looking as if he was waving. For a moment, Marie thought about phoning Josy and telling her she would keep Fluffy, but then she had to remind herself that she didn't want a dog. It didn't fit with her lifestyle, but that didn't mean she couldn't enjoy Fluffy's company for the next three weeks.

The next day, Marie's other charges arrived. Little Kelly was three years and the baby was just four months old. They were lovely children. Kelly had a soft voice and a head of bouncy blonde curls. The baby was like all babies of that age. She was soft, cuddly, smelt of baby powder and made little cooing noises. She cried when she woke but was quickly calmed with a bottle and a clean nappy. Marie always enjoyed having the girls.

Having watched Fluffy with the boys, Marie didn't feel the same level of anxiety but was still cautious when Fluffy met Kelly. Fluffy showed the same gentle affection with Kelly as he had with the boys. He showed no interest in the baby apart from a quick sniff at the pram.

Fluffy, when sat, towered above tiny Kelly, but he was so gentle. He took care to walk around her so that he didn't knock her over or push her out of the way.

By the end of the second day, Marie had completely relaxed and believed there wasn't an aggressive bone in Fluffy's body.

When Josy called that evening, Marie told her that Fluffy was a real family dog in every sense of the word. She would have no problems finding a home for such a wonderful animal. But, she warned Josy, just not her family home. Josy thought Marie didn't sound very convincing. Fluffy had clearly made a big impression on Marie in just two days. Would Marie be so keen to let him go after three weeks?

CHAPTER 10
MICHELLE AND NUMAN
THE DAWNING

Numan was true to his word and travelled to the farm where the dog attack had occurred six weeks before. He was surprised to find such a run-down, dirty property. It looked nothing like the photographs on the file. The gate was unlatched and creaked on its hinges. The farmyard showed no sign of life and looked as if it had been abandoned years ago. It was muddy. Rotting sheep manure and wet straw gave off a putrid stench.

Numan approached the door and tapped lightly, but the catch was broken and the door swung open. Numan stood for a moment, not sure whether to enter or try to knock again. The details had shown that the farmer still lived there but the place looked empty.

Then he heard a low groan, like an animal in pain. Curious, Numan stepped inside. "Jack," he called. "Jack Hawkins?"

He found Jack in the lounge, or at least that's what it had been. It bore all the remnants of a past life. A sideboard with family photographs, a comfortable suite with scatter cushions and a rug in front of an ornate stone fireplace. But now it was littered with empty beer bottles. It smelt of alcohol and vomit. And dust, everywhere—dust and dirt.

Jack was lying on the sofa, clearly drunk.

"What you want?" Jack slurred.

"I'm a police officer. My name's Numan. I need to talk to you about the…" Numan hesitated. *What was it? An accident? An incident? An attack? A murder? Which was the right word?* "I need to talk about the accident."

Jack groaned.

Numan looked down at the skinny figure on the sofa. He was clearly drunk but there seemed more. His skin was grey and his lips looked blue. The room was freezing.

"Are you ill? Should I call someone for you?"

"No one," Jack said in an anguished voice. "There's no one left."

That statement told Numan everything. Clearly, the attack had caused more than physical injuries. It was obvious that this man was deeply scarred, but his scars were not physical like Michelle's. Nonetheless, they were deep scars that would never heal.

"Jack, I know it's difficult and I'll go away if you want. But I know someone who was involved in a similar incident. I want to stop this sort of thing happening. I'm trying to understand. So if you feel up to talking, if you can tell me anything, it might just help someone else."

Jack let out a sob. He pulled himself into a sitting position. Tears streamed down his face as he began to talk. He spewed out all the information he had for an hour while Numan made notes. He told him about the beautiful woman who lived in his cottage. He told him about her delightful children, clever Michael and loving Molly. He told him about how he had hoped Michael would be placed in the junior sheepdog trials and how he had found the loving, gentle Molly on the barn floor covered in blood. He sobbed and shook with rage when he told him how he had shot his dogs and how he could never be around another dog.

Then he broke down, sobbing uncontrollably. Numan couldn't figure out a way to comfort this wretched, broken man, so he tapped him on the shoulder and said, "I am sorry. I am really so sorry. Please try to take comfort in that your bravery in talking to me will help us to understand. If we can stop just one incident, it will be one life you have helped to save. If I can do anything to help you, please let me know."

Jack sat with his head in his hands, sobbing.

Numan put his card on the arm of the settee and walked towards the door. He was in the doorway when Jack said, "I couldn't stand to be around a dog, so that's why I took Fluffy to the kennel. Fluffy hadn't done anything and he was beautiful. Beautiful, white, gentle and Molly's friend. But I couldn't be around him. Too many memories!"

Numan froze at the door. "Fluffy? Did you say Fluffy? And he was white?" Numan asked with his eyes almost out of his sockets. He turned around and sat back down.

They talked for another hour. Numan told Jack how he had got involved in the search for the big white dog. He told him about Michelle and her baby. He told him about her bravery and how she was helping him to track down vicious dogs.

At first Jack didn't believe it, couldn't comprehend it, believed it must be a mistake. But the nagging doubt crept in. His other dogs had never shown any aggression towards the children and preferred to move away rather than have anything to do with them.

Fluffy's appearance was unusual, if not unique and Jack hadn't actually seen anything. Could Fluffy be responsible? Had Jack got it all wrong? Jack showed Numan the picture of Fluffy curled up in the blankets with Michael and Molly. Surely, this dog couldn't be a killer.

"Can I take this photo?" Numan asked. "I'll bring it back. But I just want to make sure."

Jack nodded and Numan placed the photo in his pocket.

Jack sat in silence for a moment. He felt sober now. He was confused. Could he have got everything wrong?

But one thing Jack knew for sure, he needed to find the truth. He needed to know if it was Fluffy that had ruined his life and if it was, he needed to make sure Fluffy never did anything like that ever again. He deserved that much.

It was getting late. Numan told Jack he would go to the kennels tomorrow.

"I want to go with you," said Jack.

Numan looked at him doubtfully.

"Please," said Jack. "I need to know. Surely, I deserve that. I won't drink," he added as an afterthought.

Numan looked at the broken man in front of him.

"Okay," said Numan sofly. "I'll pick you up in the morning."

Once outside, Numan called Michelle. "Michelle before I say another word, please understand this could be a wild goose chase. I may have this all wrong." He hesitated, "I think I may have found the white dog."

There was a silence then a rasping sob.

"It's late, but I'll come over. I have a photo."

It was eleven at night when Numan got to Michelle's front door. She had been waiting and opened it before he knocked. Michelle's mother had gone to bed so they sat at the kitchen table while Numan told her about the events of the day.

"I could be wrong," Numan said, but his voice lacked conviction.

"You said you had a photo," Michelle hissed.

Numan pulled the photo from his pocket. Michelle stared at it. Turned it over. The dog was mostly covered in blankets, but you could see its size, head and ears.

Her heart began to pound. It was just something, something that she couldn't explain, but the dog had haunted her dreams every night. "It's him," she said, passing the photo back to Numan.

"Are you sure? He's covered up, you can hardly see…"

"It's him," Michelle had almost shouted, her voice strong. "I know it's him."

"I'll pick you up first thing," Numan put the photo back in his pocket and left Michelle sitting at the table. It was difficult to read Michelle's expression, but he thought he could feel her grief and her relief but, most of all, her anger.

"You must be wrong!" Josy was not happy. *These three people had barged into the kennels with this bizarre tale of dog attacks. And the culprit was supposed to be the dog which had been playing so well with Auntie Marie's charges. Not just tolerating them, actually playing with them, calming them, sitting with them playing teddies. They absolutely had to be wrong. And this man, Jack, he had handed the dog in just two weeks ago and made no mention of it being aggressive.*

"I thought the dogs responsible for the attack on your farm were identified and..." Josy tilted her head defiantly. "You dealt with them."

"I thought so too said Jack, but I think I may have it wrong."

"I think not," said Josy defiantly. "The dog you handed in is a family dog and has been housed with a family." This wasn't strictly true, but Josy wanted to make the point that Fluffy was indeed a family dog.

Jack, Numan and Michelle, wearing her veil, glanced at each other. Numan looked irrritated. "Look, I hope we're wrong," said Numan, "but we just need to check." Numan wasn't quite sure what he was going to check, but he didn't want this white dog out in the public domain unless he could be sure it wasn't responsible for the attacks.

Josy wasn't giving in. She always tried to protect the dogs in her care and refused to believe that particular dog could have been responsible for killing a spider, let alone a child.

"Have you got a warrant?" Josy asked. "I don't have to give you any details without a warrant."

Numan looked beaten. He could get a warrant fairly easily, but it would be a non-urgent case and may take a couple of days.

"We'll be back," he said, irritated and turned to leave. But Michelle stepped forward and lifted her veil. Josy gasped and took two steps back. This thing in front of her was barely human. Jack also had an expression of complete horror.

"And meanwhile," said Michelle calmly, "let's just pray that nothing happens to the family you've placed this dog with."

Josy hesitated. "It's my aunt," said Josy. "She lives in the town, ten minutes away. I'll take you. It will be easier. I know where it is. Give me two minutes to lock up, but please, keep an open mind. This dog is beautiful and affectionate. He may look like the dog you're looking for, but I'm sure it's not him. I'll take you there because I believe you need to know that."

A few minutes later, Josy was directing Numan to her aunt's house in the town.

Marie's life was good. She was managing life. She wasn't rich, but with her part-time childminding jobs and a legacy left by her mother, she could keep her head above water and even manage an annual holiday. She knew most people in the small town and often went for coffee and a chat with local friends. Marie enjoyed the routine. She liked to keep fit, so walking the dogs at the kennel was a good fit for Marie's lifestyle.

Her house was small but big enough for her. She had a small garden, but it was enough for the children to play outside in the warmer weather.

Marie was a good childminder. Marie was dependable and calm. She didn't mind if the children made dens in the living room, although she had sometimes wished the boys would make just one den and be just a bit quieter. It always took Marie a few hours after they left to put the house back together and recover from her headache.

The girls she cared for were just sweet children. Kelly played quietly on her own and the baby only ever cried when she was hungry or needed a clean nappy.

Marie was in the kitchen with Fluffy. The baby was asleep upstairs, but Marie had a baby alarm so that she would hear if she woke up. The living room was separated from the kitchen by just one door, so Marie could see Kelly quietly playing with the toys. Marie was preparing lunch. She looked down at Fluffy. As usual, he was by Marie's side. He wandered over to the far side of the kitchen.

Marie hummed to herself as she made sandwiches. A small piece of cheese fell onto the worktop. Without thinking, she picked it up and turned to offer it to Fluffy.

It took just a few seconds. One second he was wagging his tail and looking like the cutest ball of fluff you ever saw;

the next, he had flattened his ears, curled his lip into a snarl and growled a low, guttural, threatening growl as he looked straight at Kelly.

Marie was fast. She shot into the living room and tried to slam the door, but Fluffy was right behind her and threw his weight into the door. Somehow, Marie stood her ground. She pushed on the door with all her strength. Fluffy yelped. He must have caught his nose in the door, but the door latch caught and closed.

She knew it wouldn't hold long. Fluffy was a big dog. He was throwing himself at the door, clawing at the door, snarling, biting the door handle and the door frame.

Marie couldn't leave the door but using her foot, she managed to drag the table within reach. She turned it on its side and barricaded the door. Quickly, she moved all the furniture to the door to reinforce the barrier. She was relieved to see her mobile phone on the coffee table. Kelly had started to cry. Marie snatched her up and held her close while she dialed the emergency service number.

"Which service?" asked the operator in a monotone voice.

"I don't know," said Marie frantically. "We are being attacked by a dog. I'm barricaded into my front room. Please hurry."

"And where is the dog at the moment?" asked the operator, still sounding bored.

"It's the other side of the door," screamed Marie, "but I don't know how long it will hold. Please hurry."

"And what sort of dog is it?" the operator droned.

"I don't fucking know. I just know if I don't get help quickly, it's going to kill me. I've got a child in here." Then with the sinking realisation she said, "Oh my god, the baby. I've got a baby upstairs and he can get to the baby."

That seemed to do the trick. The operator took Marie's address and said emergency services were on their way. She told Marie to keep calm.

Marie stared at the phone. Was there anyone else who could help? A neighbour, anyone, But Marie, knew that anyone approaching Fluffy at the moment would put themselves in extreme danger.

The baby. What about the baby? But Marie was trying to protect Kelly. If she tried to leave the room she would be putting Kelly at risk.

The door would hold for a while. As long as Fluffy was focused on getting into the room, he wasn't thinking of the baby, so Marie pounded on the door.

"Come on, you bastard dog. You keep trying the door. That's right, you throw yourself at it," she tried keeping his focus. "You won't get in here, you bastard."

Suddenly, it all went quiet. Marie put her ear against the door. Nothing. Where was he? She heard the distant sounds of sirens. Then she heard Fluffy bark. She hadn't heard him bark before, but a sickening feeling swept over her as she realised that the bark had come from the baby alarm.

Fluffy was with the baby and there was nothing she could do.

Cautiously, she started to slide away the furniture from the door. She wasn't sure what to do. She couldn't think straight. Kelly was still crying and she needed to protect her.

She listened, putting her ear to the baby alarm. She could hear snuffling and sniffing. What was that? Fluffy? The baby?

The young police officer pulled his baton out of his belt and nervously approached the door. The only information he'd been given was 'Dog attack in progress.' It could be anything from a Great Dane to a Yorkshire Terrier, but the house seemed quiet.

He tried the door. It was open. He entered nervously and heard the muffled cry of a child. The noise was coming from a downstairs door. He tried the door, but it wouldn't open. It was then he saw the deep claw marks in the door. The bite marks and the blood.

"Police!" he shouted.

He heard furniture being dragged away from the door and the next minute, a disheveled young woman stood in front of him, clutching a small child and shaking.

"He's upstairs," she said in a trembling voice. "He's upstairs with the baby."

At that moment, another patrol car pulled up and another two police officers ran into the house.

"He's upstairs," indicated the first police officer. "And there's a baby up there."

He looked at the door ravaged by Fluffy's attempts to get in and wondered if there was still a live baby up there. They all pulled their batons, but no one seemed to want to go first. Then hesitating, the young policeman moved towards the stairs, closely followed by the others. All was quiet. Even Kelly had stopped crying.

As they rounded the corner, they saw two police cars and a police van.

"We're too late," said Numan. "We're too bloody late!"

As Josy brought the car to a halt, they all jumped out and rushed towards the house. A uniformed policeman was standing at the gate, barring their way. "You can't go in there." He straightened and moved into a more central position. Numan flashed his card, taking care to cover the part which indicated he was not from the area. The officer looked slightly unsure. He looked at the odd collection of people: a lady with her face hidden by a thick veil, a very thin man in a sports jacket and stained trousers that looked too big, and a young girl in what appeared to be some sort of overalls.

Numan saw him looking. "They're with me," he stated as if no other explanation was necessary.

The officer moved aside. "Injuries?" Numan asked. But the officer seemed to stutter, unsure of what to disclose. Numan ignored him and stepped quickly inside the property. Most of the noise was coming from upstairs, so Numan headed for the stairs. They all noticed the deep claw marks, blood and splinters on the living room door. But it didn't look as if the door had given way. It remained on its hinges.

Whoever had been in there had been lucky, Numan thought

He took the stairs two at a time and was greeted by an officer with a lead on a large white dog. The dog seemed completely calm and wagged its tail when it saw Numan.

"Where are you taking him?" Numan asked.

"Kennels," said the officer. "We're hoping someone can sign the notice to have him humanely destroyed."

"I'm from the kennels," said Josy, stepping forward. "I'll sign the paper right now."

Numan pushed open the door and gazed around the room. He saw a young woman clutching a young child in one arm and a baby in the other. She appeared to be shaking. "Anyone injured?" Numan asked.

"No," whispered Marie. "We're all fine."

"Thank God!" said Numan, and he meant it.

Michelle, Josy, Jack and Numan followed the police van to the veterinary surgery. The vet argued that it was better if they didn't come in but Numan showed his card and argued that the dog was likely to be calmer around people he knew.

In fact, when Fluffy saw Jack, he immediately started to pull towards him, wagging his tail excitedly.

"I'll take him," said Jack, taking the lead from the policeman, who seemed only too pleased to pass it over.

They filed through into the examination room and the vet took out a syringe and filled it from a bottle. "Its okay, Fluffy," said the vet softly. He pinched up Fluffy's skin at the back of his neck and pushed the syringe into his deep fur.

Fluffy's eyes seemed to struggle to stay open. He laid down peacefully and started to drift away. But suddenly, with a last spurt of energy, he jumped up, turned, flattened his ears with a snarl, and bit hard onto Jack's hand.

The vet, totally shocked, quickly tried to prepare another syringe while Numan tried to pull Fluffy away from Jack's hand. Before the vet could inject the second syringe, Fluffy released his grip, laid down and closed his eyes. He was gone.

Finally, Jack was able to pull his hand away, but three of his fingers were bitten through to the bone and his hand pumped blood, which pooled across the floor.

"Bloody hell!" exclaimed the vet. "In my thirty years of practice, I've never seen anything like that."

CHAPTER 11
FLUFFY'S LEGACY –
10 MONTHS ON

Victoria

Victoria and her two children had quickly forgotten about Fluffy. The children were completely taken with the smaller terrier, which she had swapped for Fluffy. He was a lively little thing and very playful. He was small, so Victoria could manage him easily.

Tommy, having received a diagnosis of autism, was now getting the education he needed to enable him to reach his full potential. Victoria knew he would never be a high-paid professional, but Tommy was doing well and developing independence.

Victoria believed that Tommy would one day be able to work and communicate with people. He already had friends and had stopped the dreadful screaming. But above all, Tommy was happy.

Laura, Victoria's older daughter, was very bright. Victoria wondered sometimes where it came from. Laura was interested in marine biology and was already talking about university. *Such an old wise head on such young shoulders,* Victoria thought.

There were no photographs of Fluffy. Even when the TV news reported a family's lucky escape at the mercy of a vicious dog, even when a picture of Fluffy flashed onto the TV no one took any notice. Victoria was making tea, Tommy was playing with toy cars and Laura had her head in a book.

The family had no idea of the monster that had been created in their home.

Jill

People who knew Jill also knew how much she missed her late husband and struggled to come to terms with his death. Because Jill had almost turned into a recluse, very few people knew she owned a dog and none knew how close she had become to him.

The people who did know, mostly delivery drivers, assumed that someone had taken the dog in, so no one asked questions.

The police continued to hunt for the dog who had killed the child close to Jill's property, but there were no leads, and after a while, the case was filed in the cold case files.

Jill had left a will instructing that her assets and business should be sold and distributed to charity. The local church was able to finish the repairs to the steeple and more besides. A significant amount of money was given to the dog rehoming centre where Jill had first met Fluffy. But poor record keeping meant that the connection was never made. It was just a nice and very useful legacy from an unknown lady.

Chris

Chris turned his life around.

After two hospital admissions for alcohol-related illness, he had met a charity worker who took him under her wing. He received medication and counselling to help him with his drinking problem. During the counselling, he referred to his friend and just said he had lost a friend under horrific circumstances. He refused to say more.

Everyone assumed that it was another homeless person who had such an effect on Chris and he never corrected them.

Man, woman, dog, it didn't matter to Chris. It had been a friend. A true friend to him. Fluffy had never hurt Chris and Chris still felt a pang of guilt at betraying him.

Chris hoped one day he might have another dog, but for now, he was living in semi-sheltered housing. He had a bedsit, a place of his own to call home. There were only a few rules: no drink, no drugs and no pets. But Chris wasn't planning to be there forever. He had a job—cleaning at a factory, but he hoped he might be able to get a different position, perhaps on the production line, where he could earn a bit more money. Then he could move, perhaps to a flat, and have a dog and normal life.

He had a goal and a dream.

Eric

Eric's body lay decomposing under a thick bush in the wood. He was never missed. In the future, someone may discover human remains and wonder who this person was and what sort of life they lived.

The skeleton would show the signs of a dog attack, or perhaps just signs of forest animals, foxes maybe, who had chewed on a collection of old bones.

No one appeared to own the bungalow and as it tumbled down out in the wilderness, no one was interested in it. If anyone had looked, they would see that it was registered to a man called Eric. But Eric had gone and in a few more years, the bungalow would be no more than a pile of bricks.

Jack

Jack wrote a letter to Katherine. He tried to explain about Fluffy. He told her how sorry he was, how much he missed her and loved her. He never received a reply.

Jack died eighteen months later. He had taken a mixture of alcohol and pills. No one knew if it was an accident or suicide. He didn't leave a note. But he was clutching a photograph of Katherine when he died.

He was found on his sofa in his squalid, dirty house. They thought he had been dead for a couple of weeks. His body was starting to smell. The stubs on his hand, had once been fingers. It seemed like they were never dressed or cleaned. The flesh around them was infected and green.

No one came to his funeral.

Katherine tried her best to start again. After six months, she moved out of her mother's house and into a flat in a nearby town. She couldn't bear for a single part of her life to be anything like the life she had lived in the farm cottage. The memories were too painful.

She didn't walk in the countryside; instead walked in a park. She didn't cook her apple pie, which Molly had loved so much, and she froze at the sight of a dog.

Michael had wanted to pursue his farming interests, but seeing how much this seemed to distress his mother he dropped it and tried to take interest in computers. He struggled with his studies.

The letter that Jack had sent remained in Katherine's drawer unopened. It was all just too painful.

Perhaps one day, but not yet.

Marie

Marie continued with her childminding business, took on more children and worked five days a week, sometimes six. She enjoyed her work and told Josy she didn't have time to volunteer at the kennel. But they both knew the real reason was that Marie would never want to be around a dog ever again. Even small dogs made Marie cringe. She crossed the street to avoid them and even threw a stuffed toy away because it seemed to resemble a dog.

Josy

Josy continued to work at the kennel. She still loved her job and still refused to put a dog down. She believed there was a home for every dog. She just had to find the right home. She had been shocked by Michelle's appearance and carried away by the events of that day. She also knew that there was very little she could have done to make the outcome any different. But she had seen Fluffy and still believed that something had triggered his behaviour. Josy still believed that the right owner and the right home could have prevented Fluffy from attacking. She thought about the facts. Had Michelle correctly identified Fluffy? Had Jack actually seen Fluffy attack?

To Josy, it all seemed circumstantial. Marie had never wanted Fluffy and Josy wondered if Fluffy knew that. When the police found Fluffy, he was sitting next to the baby's cot while the baby cooed contentedly.

"No," Josy said to herself. "He would never have hurt anyone. It must have all been some sort of big mistake."

Michelle and Numan

Numan's reputation as a dog attack expert grew and grew until he was doing little else than answering queries and helping with dog bites and attacks. Eventually, he was told to make a choice. Either he should stand down, or else he had to devote more time to the general policing he was employed to do. He resigned immediately.

To begin with, he wasn't sure what he was going to do, but the phone calls kept coming, so he set up a very lucrative business helping track vicious dogs and support dog attack victims.

Often, people who had been bitten felt so angry and distressed that they were only too happy to pay Numan to track down the culprit. Numan also picked up work from various police forces around the country. He lectured and provided training to police, local authorities and delivery services.

Michelle worked with Numan. She was a dedicated worker with a real belief in what she was doing. When they weren't tracking dogs they studied together, trying to make sense of what makes a dog attack.

Michelle was bright and Numan really wanted to have her at his side when he delivered training and lectures, but she refused to go out. She remained inside unless she had to go out for a medical visit with her thick black veil.

Michelle's mother was pleased that she had been able to find work and interest and believed she was doing okay. But deep down, Michelle would never recover. She couldn't stand to look at herself and knew no one could stand to look at her either.

The operations were unsuccessful, and in the end, Michelle refused to get more medical treatment. She knew she could never have her face back and she was always going to look like a monster.

She secretly cried herself to sleep nearly every night. She dreamed of having a relationship with a man or even just a friend—a real friend. Numan had been good to Michelle, and she thought he might care about her, but when she thought about her face, she believed no one could ever really love her the way she was.

And there was George. Dear sweet little George who Michelle had failed to protect. Why was she alive and not George?

To her mother and Numan, she appeared to be coping. But Michelle would remain locked in her own secret nightmare for the rest of her life.

Puppies

The puppies were born in the kennel. Bella, the German Shepherd, had no problems giving birth, although Josy kept a close eye.

They were cute; two of them looked like Bella and one was pure white. Josy knew she would have no problem homing them and sure enough, they were offered homes as soon as they were weaned.

The German Shepherd lookalikes were found homes close to the town. One was in a local pub and the other went to a couple with grown-up children.

The little white puppy had been spotted on the internet by a couple living over a hundred miles away. They were so keen that they had made numerous trips to the kennel to visit the puppy before he was ready to leave Bella.

Now, they watched the puppy as he played contentedly on the floor of their living room with the numerous toys they had bought him.

"He's so cute," said the woman. "I adore him!"

At that moment, the puppy stared at the toy, ears flattened against its head. The puppy's expression changed so suddenly and he savagely bit into the toy. He shook it so violently it split in half.

The couple looked at each other for a moment in shock. But the puppy seemed to return to its playful demure.

"He's just playing," said the woman. "I'll make a cup of tea."

ACKNOWLEDGEMENT

ABOUT THE AUTHOR

Vera Shilling lost her sight following an antibiotic resistant infection. Vera had always enjoyed writing and after learning to use the computer in a different way, she continued to write.

She works in a number of voluntary roles and has been nominated for awards for her work. Life continues to provide challenges and Vera says she learns something differently every day.

Her goal is to live a full and independent life and to be an example to other sight impaired people as to what can be achieved.